RAPUNZELS AND POWERS

BOOK 10 OF THE FAIRY TALES OF THE MAGICORUM

CHRISTINA BAUER

COPYRIGHT

Newton, MA 02464
www.monsterhousebooks.com
ISBN 978-1-956114-45-4

DEDICATION

**For All Those Who Kick Ass, Take Names
and Read Books**

CONTENTS

BONUS IMAGES

COLLECTED WORKS

Fairy Tales of the Magicorum

Modern fairy tales with sass, action, and romance

1. Wolves and Roses
2. Moonlight and Midtown
3. Shifters and Glyphs
4. Slippers and Thieves
5. Bandits and Ball Gowns
6. Fire and Cinder
7. Fairies and Frosting
8. Towers and Tithes
9. Mirrors and Mysteries
10. Rapunzels and Powers

Witches of the Magicorum

1. Evil Queens and Goblin Kings

2. Mad Hatters and Manhattan Heirs

3. Goose Girls and Ghost Magic

Angelbound Origins

About a quasi (part demon and part human) girl who loves kicking butt in Purgatory's Arena

1. Angelbound
2. Scala
3. Acca
4. Thrax
5. The Dark Lands
6. The Brutal Time
7. Armageddon
8. Quasi Redux
9. Clockwork Igni
10. Lady Reaper
11. Reaper Games
12. Angry Gods

Angelbound Lincoln

The Angelbound experience as told by Prince Lincoln

1. Duty Bound
2. Lincoln
3. Trickster
4. Baculum
5. Angelfire

6. Rixa

7. Mordred

Angelbound Offspring

The next generation takes on Heaven, Hell, and everything in between

1. Maxon

2. Portia

3. Zinnia

4. Rhodes

5. Kaps

6. Mack

7. Huntress

** This is a completed series.*

Angelbound Xavier

Xavier's story

1. Archenemy

2. Archnemesis

3. Archangel

Pixieland Diaries

Sassy pixie Calla loves elf prince Dare. Too bad he hasn't noticed her. Yet.

1. Pixieland Diaries

2. Calla

3. Dare
This is a completed series.

Dimension Drift

Dystopian adventures with science, snark, and hot aliens
1. Scythe
2. Umbra
3. Alien Minds
4. ECHO Academy

This is a completed series.

Beholder

Where a medieval farm girl discovers necromancy and true love
1. Cursed
2. Concealed
3. Cherished
4. Crowned
5. Cradled

This is a completed series.

RAPUNZELS AND POWERS

Dex's Cabin

GRAYSON

SEVENTEEN YEARS OLD

Pop! A bubbling noise wakes me up. Blinking, I focus my sleepy thoughts. *Where am I again?*

Pop, pop!

Oh, that's right. Hours ago, Dex and I dozed off in his cabin. Now we're resting nose-to-nose under heavy blankets.

Maybe it's from being a wolf shifter, but Dex is an expert cuddler. He angles his left arm so it serves as my pillow. At the same time, Dex cups the back of my head with his right hand. I sense every other place where we touch. *Chest. Hips. Thighs.* Although Dex remains asleep, he gently strokes the edge of my ear with his thumb. The moment is too perfect to shatter.

So, I won't.

After all, I probably dreamt those sounds anyway. Closing my eyes, I try snoozing again.

Pop, pop, pop!

Ugh. That was no dream.

Reopening my eyes, I stifle a groan. There's no mistaking that series of noises. *A magic mirror is appearing nearby.* And I know this stuff, too. My people are osmos fae. We make the best magic mirrors in all of Faerie.

It almost hurts to remove Dex's arm from over my shoulder, but I gently slide his limb aside. Dex's cabin is made from rough-hewn wood. The bedroom is a small space that holds a mattress as well as a few armoires for clothes. Since Dex rules more than a hundred shifter pups, he goes into *lone wolf mode* sometimes. This place is his retreat.

Sure enough, I spot a new mirror on the far wall. The frame shifts between green and red, which means it's not only magical, it's also meant for communication and seeing the future. My guess? Someone from the past wants to reach Dex. Which makes sense, considering how he's the Alpha of the Wulfhelm pack.

A memory appears. I picture a painting from the house of Professor Tallon, the Wulfhelm Rune Druid: it shows the pack during a werewolf commitment ceremony. In other words, a shifter wedding. A shiver twists down my back. Since Dex is a werewolf—and I'm his mate—this ritual requires that Dex and I bind our souls by biting each other's shoulders.

And that's just for starters.

As leaders of Wulfhelm, Dex and I must also recharge the pack lands with magic. Otherwise, our population of young shifter orphans will be destroyed by a nasty elf called the Prism Master and my just-as-evil sister, Lady R. Worry tightens up my neck. Fighting evil fae? Casting mega spells? That isn't me. I'm the girl who spent her life locked up in a cabin-prison. Icy alarm chills my soul.

Stay calm, Grayson.

This new mirror must be another message from Professor Tallon. What's the harm in that? Once Dex takes a look, it will all vanish.

Which means I need to wake Dex up. Such a shame.

Dex opens his right eye. "Don't worry about disturbing me."

"How'd you guess?"

"When you've been with your fated mate as long as I have, you just know."

I smile. "It has been all of ten hours."

"Nine hours and forty-seven minutes since we agreed to official coupledom, but who's counting?"

Dex is a wolf shifter. Although I'm osmos—that's part fae and troll—I'm still Dex's fated mate. Although I do feel wolfy sometimes, I won't take my beastly shape until Dex and I exchange bites. Every once in a while, that idea seems exciting.

As of this moment? Not so much.

"A new mirror has appeared," I declare. "I think it's from Professor Tallon."

"Better check it out." Dex slides out of bed. He looks beyond handsome in a pair of leather pants and nothing else. Dex is tall and broad-shouldered with long dark hair, a full mouth and a strong jawline. I'm still in my calico dress from yesterday. I've red hair, green eyes, freckles, and a slight frame. In elf-world, that makes me hella plain.

Rising from bed, I move to stand before the mirror. Once there, I realize my mistake. Because of a blindness spell, Dex can't see where I've gone.

"Do you need help finding the mirror?" I ask.

Dex shakes his head. "Lady R may have taken my vision, but her spell doesn't block anything magical."

Sadly, my awful sister cast a blinding spell on Dex. Although you wouldn't know it based on how Dex confidently strides across the room. When he pauses before me, Dex is so tall, I must tilt up my head to see his face.

Little by little, Dex reaches out to touch the pendant around my neck. "I detect more than what hangs on the wall. This mirror pendant holds your magic. I can see it, too."

Part of me is thrilled that Dex can detect my spell. More is freaked out that I made this jewelry in the first place.

This little mirror pendant magically entraps two people: First, there's Dex's Beta, Taryn, who's perma-stuck in a half-shifted state between man and wolf. Second, there's the witch, Jocasta, who always waits in the shadows. I didn't mean to imprison them—and I'm not sure how to get them out—but at least they're alive. Otherwise, Taryn and Jocasta would've died in a fire.

Where the pendant should show a reflection, a small scene plays out instead: Taryn sleeps in what looks like the Bartlebee—that's the cabin-prison of my childhood—while a dim figure sets bandages on his many burns. *Jocasta.* Not sure where this version of the Bartlebee came from, but then again, I don't know how I got these two into a mirror pendant to begin with

Pop, Pop!

The new wall-mirror grows larger until it's almost as big as Dex himself. The reflective surface shows white mist, which means the mirror is still forming.

"How much longer before we see anything?" asks Dex.

Growing up, the Prism Master forced magic mirrors to appear in the Bartlebee. Tutors showed up in the reflections… eventually. I've a lot of experience in waiting for mirrors to come into focus.

"Every mirror is different." I scan the surface. "This one has a way to go. Either the caster is very junior… or they're really far away."

Dex brushes his fingers along the mirror's heavy frame. "I can see the magic inside the wood—it keeps changing from green to red. What does that mean?"

"Osmos mirror magic has four levels. The first and easiest type is colored saffron yellow. It lets you see the past."

"And that only makes mirrors?"

"Saffron power can also make a kind of mist bomb. When you chuck it at someone, you'll erase their memory." A weight of sorrow settles inside my bones. When I next speak, my voice breaks. "That's how Lady R wiped out my life before the Bartlebee. I don't remember a thing before six years old."

"You'll get those recollections back," says Dex, his voice low and soothing. "Just like I'll regain my sight."

My throat tightens. Lady R is so powerful and determined. Even worse, she's set on destroying me and taking Dex as her so-called prince. How can we hope to stop her, not to mention her partner in crime, the Prism Master?

Focus, Grayson. Think about the mirror.

I clear my throat. "The second level of osmos magic is colored emerald. This green power makes mirrors which allow you to talk to someone in the present. You can also them to spy on people." I can't help it. My face burns red at the memories of all the times I spied on Dex. He can't see that, though.

Dex inhales. "You're embarrassed."

Then again, maybe Dex doesn't need to see—his shifter sense of smell does all the work. I'm not used to someone reading me so closely. I clear my throat again and keep going. "Level three is crimson magic. It shows the future. The fourth and final level is silver power. It can be used for almost anything. Only the osmos king or queen—the quintessence—can wield that energy."

A long pause follows while Dex keeps inhaling. I sense he's debating whether to push me on the spying thing. In the end, he keeps with my change of subject.

"So, flipping between green and red means the magic is moving between the present and future… for whoever's casting this mirror. How long before we see them?"

Inside the mirror frame, the white haze gets heavier. "If my guess is right, they'll show up in a few seconds."

Sure enough, the haze clears. An image comes into focus, showing a great green door in a darkened room. Inch by inch, the entrance swings open. A girl peeps out. She's a fae whose red hair is tied back into puffy pigtails. There's no missing her special combination of green eyes and a heart-shaped face. My pulse thuds so hard, I feel the beat against my rib cage.

The mirror shows me. And I'm six years old.

My skin prickles with shock. I don't remember anything before I woke up in the Bartlebee. And the green door in this mirror? The Bartlebee doesn't have anything like that.

An electric realization moves through my mind. This is no message from Professor Tallon. It's outreach with my younger self. Questions zing through my mind.

How could I wield any magic back then, let alone cast something so complex?

Someone must be helping Young Me create this mirror...who?

And most of all, why am I seeing it now?

GRAYSON

2

DEX

TWENTY YEARS OLD

A young Grayson appears in the mirror's reflection. She's all knobby knees, puffy hair and a determined gaze. I can't help but smile.

"That's you as a child." I state. "You're perfect."

Grayson takes a half-step backward. "I don't understand. The mirror should show Professor Tallon."

Inhaling, I catch the tang of sweat on the air. *Grayson's afraid.*

My heart sinks. My vita has been through so much. For years, the Prism Master and Lady R teamed up to bring Grayson down. Now my vita must help save Wulfhelm. I know Grayson can handle it, but that isn't enough.

She needs to know it.

Inside the mirror, Young Grayson steps into a massive dome-shaped room. The floor is a large cross-section of a tree trunk, while the dome itself is all packed dirt accented by thorny roots. A mismatched collection of mirrors lie embedded in the walls.

I remember this place. It's the same ceremonial chamber where pack Alpha Ishir and Osmos Queen Xao tried to recharge the magic of Wulfhelm. Sadly, Lady R and the Prism Master sabotaged the ceremony. Both Xao and Ishir died.

Why is young Grayson in such a dangerous spot?

The ceremonial chamber looks intact. Young Grayson must be visiting before Lady R and the Prism Master destroyed everything. The realization makes my inner wolf growl with anger. Young Grayson could still be at risk.

I gesture to the mirror. "That's the ceremonial chamber we saw before."

Grayson's eyes are glassy. "I'm not sure that's a good thing."

Grayson's scent of sweat and fear grows stronger. I move to stand behind her. Inch by inch, I wrap my arms around her waist, guiding her back to rest against my chest. Leaning in, I whisper in her ear. "You don't know this yet, but you're a match for anything."

Grayson exhales. "Keep talking like that, and I just might begin to believe it."

In the mirror's reflection, Young Grayson clears her throat. "Hello."

A voice sounds in the distance. "How did you get in here?"

My shifter hearing makes it easy for me to recognize the second speaker. "That's Queen Xao."

Grayson's spine stiffens against me. "You're right."

While the mirror focuses on Young Grayson, Queen Xao continues to speak from a distance. "You may return to the practice room, Grayson. I'll join you there to look at your casting."

"But the mirror's in here with me."

"What?"

Queen Xao steps into the mirror's reflection. She's a tall woman with strong limbs and pointed ears. Each scar on her face represents a powerful mirror that she's created. In her right hand, Xao holds a rose. Life in the Faerie Realm is strange, but that rose is especially odd.

Why would Xao tote around a flower? I make a note to ask Grayson about that later on.

Xao leans around the mirror's frame, as if she's looking for hidden wires. When she next speaks, it's half to herself.

"However did you manage that?"

Young Grayson screws up one side of her mouth. "Manage what?"

"Getting this mirror in here."

"Oh, I got tired of waiting so I asked it to follow me." Young Grayson stares at Xao in the way children do when they think their elders are missing something that's beyond obvious. "Isn't that what you do?"

"Not exactly." Xao places her palms on the mirror. "You cast this. You."

Young Grayson shrugs. "Me."

Xao's not the only one who's surprised. I can't believe what I'm seeing, either. Somehow, Young Grayson conjured a mirror that cut through time in order to send her older self a message.

This changes everything.

Based on the failed ritual by Ishir and Xao, I figured we'd need a group of osmos and shifters in order to recharge the magic of Wulfhelm. That could take years. But, if Grayson's a magical prodigy, then anything is possible and soon. Pride and excitement churn through me. My inner wolf wants to howl with joy.

The Faerie Realm is already filled with wonders.

Yet Grayson rises above them all.

XAO

3

GRAYSON

y head feels woozy. *I cast a complex spell when I was six?* There must be another reason why this mirror was following Young Me around.

Some part of me whispers that actually, I wield a ton of magic. It's got a high-pitched and musical voice. Must be my elfy side. Then, the part of me that's a troll grumbles that if I'm so powerful, then why didn't I cast a spell to escape the Bartlebee?

Good point, inner troll.

Back in the reflection, Xao finishes inspecting the mirror. "Who cast this?"

A better question I couldn't ask myself.

Young Me gives Xao the side eye. "I did."

Minutes pass as Xao does more tests. Some involve

tapping her rose wand against the mirror frame. Other times, Xao puts her hand right into the reflection itself. After a while, the queen steps back and makes an announcement.

"Well, that settles it."

I exhale. *Here it comes.* Xao will state that Young Me didn't cast this mirror. It's something from my sister, Opal.

That's not what happens.

Xao looks at Young Me and smiles. "You did cast this. How amazing."

All of a sudden, it's hard for me to pull in enough air. "That can't be right."

"Breathe, Grayson." Dex slowly runs his palms up and down my arms. His touch is warm and centering.

Off in the mirror, Young Me screws up her face in the way that kids do when they're convinced an adult is full of it. "Huh. I just did what you said."

Xao tilts her head. "I asked you to wait in the reception room."

"Yeah. And then you added, *I need a vision mirror.*"

"Oh, I'm afraid I was just talking out loud. I didn't mean for you to do anything."

"It's no big deal." Young Me waves her hand. "Opal's been leaving her school books around out root heart home. The other day, I read how to cast a vision mirror, so that's what I did."

Xao narrows her eyes. "Opal said her books have been stolen, that's why she's behind on her magic. I expected *her* to be the one casting this mirror."

Young Me's eyes widen. "Oh, I'm sure she can cast a vision mirror. Opal's the next quintessence. If she left her books around, it's because she knows this stuff already."

"Ah," says Xao slowly. "And the mirror is recording this for you to see later on in life. Is *that* what you asked it to do?"

"Nah, I just asked the mirror for help. That's what everyone does when you wish on a magic mirror, right?"

When Xao next speaks, her voice carries the same one I use while quizzing my pup students. "Tell me more."

"Only humans ask for specific things," states Young Me. "If you go off and demand stuff from a magic mirror, then it gets insulted and turns your wish into a curse." Young Me frowns. "Only…"

"What's wrong?" asks Xao.

"I was hoping the mirror would show me where I can find more lupine pups to fix."

Xao does a double take. "You cast healing spells on lupines?"

"Sure. Elise helps me find them. Then, I do the rest."

Back in the cabin, I do a double take as well. Elise the Harpy regularly brought lupines to the Bartlebee for me to heal. She said she got a vision that I could help, but it's also possible that Elise knew me from before.

Or did she have a magic mirror of her own? Unlikely. Having your own mirror is way too much power for a regular harpy like Elise.

"Let's see how much you know." Over in the mirror, Xao gestures across the room. "What type of mirror is that one?"

"Another vision mirror," answers Young Me.

"And the next three in line?"

"The first is *Queen Loreli's Bane*. Its magic can stop anyone from going in or out of Faerie. It can block mirrors, too. The next one is the *Tzar's Ire*. It releases poison on your enemies. And the last one is the most powerful. *King Korfu's snare.* You pull someone into a mirror world."

Back in the cabin, I set my hand onto the pendant which holds Taryn and Jocasta. Before I had no idea how I created such a thing. Now, I wonder…

"And have you created a mirror world?" asks Xao carefully.

"Opal left behind a book about them." Young Me twists her hands together at her waist. "I haven't told my parents about any of this. Mum and Dad don't even know I read Opal's books. I'd get in so much trouble if they found out."

"But…" prompts Xao.

Young Me half mumbles her reply. "I did cast a mirror world once."

Once again, I brush my fingers across the pendant at my throat. *I definitely knew how to do this as a kid.* I don't remember anything about Opal's books, but the spell came back when I needed it. That's how it works with human amnesia, too. Someone can know how to ride a bike but not recall the parents who taught them the skill.

Xao nods slowly. "I see."

"Am I in trouble?"

"Not yet."

"I'll tell my parents about the books, I promise."

"Allow me to do that. You won't be in trouble."

"Good. Can you tell them I see a wolf boy in a mirror sometimes? I want to hang up some pictures that I drew of him. It doesn't feel right to hide them."

Dex gives me a gentle squeeze. "By the way, I'm loving this."

Somehow, Dex can always make me smile. "I'll just stand here and pretend I'm not embarrassed."

Dex nips my ear. "Good plan."

"A wolf boy," repeats Xao. "That makes sense. I'll pass

along your request. I may have a gift for your parents as well: a pendant they can use in case of an emergency."

The pendant. The night Lady R kidnapped me, my parents used a pendant from Queen Xao to help me keep more of my memory. Maybe that's another reason why I could cast this mirror.

Back in the mirror, Young Me scrunches up her face with a look of childish confusion. "Not to be rude, your Highness, but my sister is waiting outside. You should talk to her. She's the next quintessence. I'm not."

Part of me wants to exclaim, *that's right! I'm in complete agreement with Young Me!* Xao may be Queen of the Osmos, but that doesn't mean she never makes mistakes.

That elfin voice in the back of my head pipes up again. This time, she says that *I'm* the one who's mistaken. The moment that voice rises, my troll side cuts her off. Seeing myself as powerful means reweaving the very fabric of my life. I've enough trouble adjusting to the whole idea of needing to bite Dex and recharge the magic of Wulfhelm. Ruling all the osmos as quintessence is total overload.

Back in the mirror, Queen Xao lifts her chin. "Your sister has already received plenty of my help in learning how to cast mirrors. You're the one who's new to me. Until you cast this—" here, she gestures toward the mirror's reflection "—I didn't know what you could do."

Young Me narrows her eyes at Xao. "What's really going on here?"

A jolt of surprise runs through me. Young Me is aggressive and confident. That's unexpected.

"I've an important ritual coming up," explains Xao. "My mate, Ishir, and I have spent years tinkering with a ceremony to recharge the magic of Wulfhelm."

"You mean, the place with all the wolf-shifters?"

"That's the one. It's protected by magical green fire, but the flames are getting too low. Ishir and I will recharge it."

Young Me's mouth constricts into a small o-shape. "I get it. You need a back-up plan in case things go wrong." Young Me nods toward the mirror. "That's why you wanted a vision mirror."

"Yes," confirms Xao. "It seems the mirror has answered my wish. In case of trouble at the ritual, the mirror is sending a message to your own future. Now, you must finish the spell."

"How?"

"Look into the mirror," answers Xao gently. "Words will appear. Read the message aloud and your future self will receive it. Does that makes sense?"

"Sure." Young Me does as instructed. When she next

speaks, her voice has a dreamy tone. "Make a wish of the osmos three."

"There," Xao pats Young Me's shoulder. "You just made your first prophecy."

"That was fun!" Young Me blinks. "And the osmos three are the first magic mirrors ever made! I can't wait to wish on them!"

"That won't be necessary for years and years," says Xao. "Those mirrors aren't safe for you to visit yet."

In the mirror before me and Dex, the image starts to haze over. Young Me notices as well. She steps closer to the reflection. "The mirror is fading."

"That's fine," explains Xao. "It means the wish is complete."

I turn the prophecy over in my mind. *Make a wish from the osmos three.*

That is confusing on so many levels, I don't even know where to start. Xao is right; it isn't safe to visit those mirrors. Making a wish from the osmos three is a magical suicide pact, not a quest.

I straighten my shoulders and redouble my focus. I got away from Lady R and the Prism Master. Maybe I'm not the next Osmos Queen or a super-powerful magic user. Still, I'm not the type to give up, either.

Besides, I'm here with Dex. That's got to count for something.

DEX

4

DEX

I keep Grayson in my arms, loving the solid feel of her as we both process everything that just happened.

"I don't know about you," I say, my voice low. "But, I'm in no rush to visit the osmos three."

Grayson chuckles. "Same here. Every once in a while, someone gets the bright idea to wish on those mirrors by visiting the original Snow White, Alice in Wonderland and Rapunzel. Many go on the quest. None return. I hope we never go."

"In that case, let's return to the pack and get a meal." As if in reply, Grayson's stomach grumbles. "I'll take that as a sign of agreement."

Grayson sighs. "I wish I had a fresh change of clothes before we leave."

My chest warms with pride. It makes me feel beyond good to know I can provide for my mate. "Check the yellow armoire."

Grayson steps out of my embrace. Because of the blindness spell, the world around me is darkness, save for the small orb of light that's Grayson's pendant. I hear the pit-pat of Grayson's steps as she approaches the armoire. Long creaks sound as Grayson opens the closet door, followed by a jangle of hangers as she looks through what's inside.

"This is filled with outfits," announces Grayson breathlessly. "Everything's in my size." More jangles sound, followed by the rustle of fabric. "Oh, here are some brown leathers. I've always wanted to wear something like this. When did these get here?"

"I've had that armoire ready for weeks now. It's the wolf in me. I knew you were my fated mate from the moment you fell through the Prism Master's ceiling. I couldn't have you near without caring for you."

"Which is why you've been packing my food."

"Yes, among other things."

Grayson steps up to me and winds her arms around my neck. "Thank you."

Running my palms up Grayson's back, I inhale the scent of her excitement: musk and cinnamon. I lean in closer, pausing when my lips are a breath above hers.

Grayson closes the distance between us, her mouth meeting mine in a slow kiss. Desire heats my blood.

Somehow, I break the kiss. "If we don't stop now, we'll miss breakfast with the pack."

"You're right, we should go." Grayson touches her pendant. "The pups will already be wondering what happened to Taryn and Jocasta. We need to explain."

My heart soars. "That was the first time you spoke like the vita of our pack." I brush a gentle kiss across her mouth.

"Well." There's no mistaking the sound of a smile in Grayson's voice. "Those pups get under your skin easily."

"That they do." It hurts to step away, but I end our embrace. "I'll meet you outside."

I stride across the threshold to the forest beyond. Since this is my home territory, I know every inch. The cabin stands behind me. An oak forest stretches out beyond the building. Before me, the wide clearing ends in a cliff that overlooks my lands. Focusing my inner magic, I change into my beast form. Since I'm the Alpha Brutus of the Wulfhelm pack, that means I become a twelve-foot tall giant of a wolf.

Grayson soon joins me outside. At this point, it's a routine for me to lie down so she can climb on my back. Once she's in place, I inhale the smell of pack leathers combined with Grayson's own cinnamon scent. For a moment, everything is right in the world.

"Ready?" I ask.

"Absolutely."

I take off. Wulfhelm includes large woods as well as a human-style city that sits atop a hill. My own house, Thornfield, is located inside the town itself. Time was, the pack was so large, we filled both the city and surrounding woods. These days, our pack counts around a hundred members. Most are young orphans who stay in the forest.

As I near the pack, the crisp night air changes to the dry heat of early morning. Although I can't see the sky, I can still picture the moon fading over my home.

Now that I head toward the other wolves, my body goes on high alert. As alpha of the pack, I only feel calm and complete when everyone is together.

Can't wait for it to happen again.

Even better, it will be my first time greeting the others with Grayson as the official keeper of my heart.

WULFHELM

5

GRAYSON

By now, it's second nature for me to ride on Wolf Dex's back. When the ground is flat, I can sit straight-backed and enjoy the view of Wulfhelm's hefty oaks. The branches arch overhead. Wide green leaves shift with every breeze.

Plus, Wulfhelm forest is home to more than shifters. Crimson cap brownies burrow around the dead leaves and tree roots, their tiny mushroom hats bobbing about the forest floor. Every so often, lady naiads step out from a tree trunk. They wear white cobweb gowns that shimmer against the rough bark of their skin. Far overhead, orchid fairies fly in intricate patterns that remind me of pink ribbons that wind through the clouds.

The view is so lovely, I soon forget any trouble with

mirrors and prophecies. The air fills with the scent of dried leaves and melting chocolate.

The pack is near.

We head for a specific clearing outside the city walls. A great oak stands in the center of the space. The Muster Tree. The sky is still lightening with dawn, so it's dark enough for magic lanterns to shine from the hefty branches.

"Here's the best part," says Wolf Dex. "I'll now call the pack without saying a word."

Wolf Dex closes his eyes. Waves of energy rise from his body. The power is undetectable to non-shifters, but I feel it keenly. Warmth rolls through my limbs. An overpowering urge overtakes my thoughts.

Get close to your alpha.

It's a reflex to lie down on Dex's back, feeling his soft fur brush against my exposed skin.

Yips and high-pitched howls sound from the nearby woods. The pups feel the same pull. A hundred of them charge out from the forest to race around the Muster Tree. A handful of older wolf shifters totter out with the pack.

I scan the many pups, looking for my students. Most of the orphans here are boys. I teach the six girls of Wulfhelm.

The city wall is lined with entrances and exits. One of those heavy wooden doors swings open. My students all march out in a neat line. They're in their human form, complete with new dresses that actually fit. They've braided their hair with ribbons. Even better, each one holds a different book.

I slide off Wolf Dex's back and rush over to my girls. They all smile and wave as I approach.

"Good morning, Miss Grayson!" They chant in unison.

My girls surround me in a group hug. My soul warms. When I first arrived, the girls didn't see any value in human stuff like clothes or learning. This display is a reward beyond anything I expected.

Although she's not the tallest or oldest girl, Hiriah remains the clear leader of this group. She wears a yellow dress that highlights her amber skin and long black hair. Her lupine pup, Snowball, follows behind her.

After our greetings, we join the rest of the pack. Although Wolf Dex is still unable to see, he still turns his furry head in my direction and winks. No doubt, he can scent that I'm overjoyed.

I stand beside Wolf Dex and the Muster Tree. The pack arrays around us in a great circle. I still can't get used to the size of Wolf Dex. I lean against his front leg.

No one else moves. A breathless kind of energy hangs in the air. Everyone stares at me and Wolf Dex. I'd guess the pack could tell there was interest between us before. Now, we're clearly a couple.

Wolf Dex does that thing where he twists his head almost one hundred and eighty degrees to look at me. The question is there if unasked, *Do you want to say anything?*

I nod. *Yes.*

Dex winks again. *Go for it.*

"Hello, everyone." Since I was a kid, I'd imagined announcing to everyone that I was now dating my wolf-boy. I even planned a few speeches. Now, all those words vanish from my brain. "I… well… Dex and I are officially a couple."

Wolf Ulliver trots out from the pack. He looks like a mini version of Dex, which means his animal is strong limbed and bright eyed. Like Dex, Ulliver can also speak in his wolf form.

"Are you our vita?" asks Ulliver.

"Duh," says Hiriah. "Grayson and Dex haven't gone through the ceremony yet."

"They could just bite each other," counters Ulliver.

The rest of the pups yip or run about in circles. Since they're still in their human forms, the rest of my girls start talking at once.

"No, they have to fix Wulfhelm's magic first."

"But Grayson could already have a bite on her shoulder."

"I want to see her cast a spell."

"She's already our vita. You don't need that."

Wolf Dex sits back on his haunches, a move that makes his already-huge form look even bigger. "Quiet down, everyone." The way Wolf Dex speaks these words, the entire pack becomes silent. "Do you have another question, Ulliver?"

In other words, Wolf Dex is done with this topic. No complaints here.

Wolf Ulliver tilts his head, considering. "What happened to Beta Taryn?"

"There was a fire a few days ago," says Wolf Dex. "It rook down Thornfield's tower."

"Oh, we saw that," says Hiriah. "The fire's out but everything still smells like smoke."

"Beta Taryn was in that tower and protecting a witch named Jocasta," I explain. "I used magic to put them both in this." I tap the pendant. "They're safe in here."

Hiriah steps closer. "Do you know how to get them out?"

One thing about wolf shifters—they can all scent a lie. "Not yet," I answer.

Hiriah pauses before me. "May I see?"

"Sure." I take off te pendant and hold it in my palms.

The rest of the pack stays in place. Wolf Ulliver trots over to have a look at well. I glance into the pendant itself. Taryn is still in bed with Jocasta standing nearby.

Ulliver and Hiriah share a long look before speaking one work in unison. "Okay."

With that, the conversation seems to be over. That fact warms my heart. *Dex has done a good job with these kids. They trust that the adults who care for them will do the right thing for others.*

I scan the adult teachers in the back of the crowd. Although they're much older, pack hierarchy depends on power, not age. Outside of Taryn and Dex, Ulliver and Hiriah are the two most dominant members.

Hiriah nods at the pendant. "That's a cool spell."

"Did you say when you'll recharge the green magic of Wulfhelm?" asks Ulliver.

"No," says Wolf Dex.

Hiriah rolls her eyes. "Grayson can do better than green. I bet she can turn Wulfhelm fire crimson, or maybe even silver!"

Dex's eyes widen. "Silver osmos magic," he repeats. "How do you know about that?"

Hiriah grips her book more closely against her chest.

"We found some books in that old creepy house with the marks on the door."

"The old rune druid's place?" I ask.

Hiriah winces. "What?"

"The house of Professor Tallon," clarifies Dex.

"Yes, that's the one," confirms Hiriah. "We found stuff about osmos magic. We put them back though." She looks down at the book she's holding. "This one's about puppies."

Hiriah goes on to talk about the best ways to feed and care for pups. I pretend to listen. In reality, the world takes on a dreamlike sheen.

My girl pups found books about osmos magic.

I didn't realize any still existed. That said, it makes sense. Xao and Ishir spent years creating a ceremony to recharge Wulfhelm. Professor Tallon would have helped in that. Hope sparks in my chest.

What else does Master Tallon have in his library?

"Thank you," says Dex. "This concludes today's pack business. Why don't you two find Teacher Clements and ask him to come over?"

Hiriah and Wolf Ulliver skip off and do as asked. A few minutes later, an older teacher with wrinkled skin and flinty eyes steps over. He's now out of his wolf form and wearing a saggy gray suit. A halo of white hair encircles his head.

"You asked for me, Alpha?" asks Clements.

"What were the pups doing in town?" asks Dex. "They're not supposed to run around there alone."

"Apologies, Alpha," says Clements. "Without Taryn around, they do tend to run a little wild."

"Ah." Wolf Dex nods. "I understand. Do your best. We'll get Taryn back soon."

"I hope so," says Clements. "For now, it's time for the pups to swim. Would you like to join us?"

Wolf Dex looks to me. "What do you say?"

"I'd rather see those books at Professor Tallon's house." I absently run my fingers across the pendant. "Perhaps there's something there to help Taryn and Jocasta."

"Good idea." Wolf Dex turns to Clements. "We'll join you for a swim another time."

Once the teachers and pack are gone, I'm anxious to visit Professor Tallon's house. My stomach decides that now is a great time to rumble again at top volume. Dex doesn't miss it, of course. He convinces me to enjoy another meal of cheese sandwiches, which he makes himself.

After that, the pups and teachers approach us with questions. Now that the girls are acting more human, the boys want the same, too. We need to find them books, beds, and human-style clothes that fit. Considering we have ninety-odd boys in the pack, this takes some time.

It seems we're in the middle of a style revolution. And it all started when the girls marched up to the Muster Tree with their books and ribbons.

MUSTER TREE

6

DEX

As part of finding the boy pups new human clothes, I show Grayson the armoires of outfits I have for her in Thornfield. She changes into a lovely red silk shirt and dark pants. I change into my pack formal leathers.

It's well after the pups fall asleep in Thornfield before Grayson and I finally head out to Professor Tallon's library. It's sweet to share a nighttime walk through the city. Insects chirp. Owls hoot. A gentle breeze rustles the leaves on the walkways. All in all, the place doesn't seem so much empty anymore as resting.

As we step along, Grayson keeps checking her mirror pendant. Although I'm struck by a blindness spell, I can still see that round mirror. Tiny images of

Taryn and Jocasta reflect through the darkness. The two seem fine, but I scent worry coming from Grayson.

"I've a question for you," I begin.

Grayson still cradles the pendant in her palms. "Sure."

"When the mirror showed up in my cabin, Xao asked a younger version of you about mirror worlds. You told her you'd cast one before."

"That's right."

"What happened?"

"Oh." A sickly-sweet scent traces on the air. Grayson is embarrassed.

"You don't have to discuss it."

"Good." Grayson sighs. "Until Xao asked about it, I'd forgotten all about casting a mirror world." She sighs. "What a disaster."

The scent of Grayson's embarrassment turns stronger. *This is too interesting to drop.* "Now, I have to know."

"You won't drop this, will you?"

"Never."

"Back when I was a kid, I snuck a book about mirror worlds out from Opal's room. It was forbidden to even enter my sister's room, let alone touch her stuff. In my defense, there were no kids in my neighborhood to play with."

"No need to defend," I state. "You had me at *snuck out a book to read*. You've seen my library. I'm more than a pretty face and some fangs."

Grayson giggles. *I do love to make her laugh.* "In that case," she continues, "I take back the stuff about defending my reading."

"Quite right."

"Back to the story. I'm a kid in my room inside our root heart. Oh, did I mention I lived in a root heart home? They're carved out of the stumps of massive and then stuck in a troll cave. It's where we elfy-trolls live."

"I did know this already. Are you stalling, Grayson?"

"Only a lot."

"The story is killing me. Do go on."

"Fine. I'm reading a book about mirror worlds and I think, wouldn't it be nice if Glubby the goldfish had his own world… instead of being stuck in a bowl?"

It's very hard to keep a straight face, but I somehow manage it. "You had a goldfish named Glubby?"

"Sure. My parents went on vacation to the human world and brought back a very non-magical Glubby for me. Since there were no kids around for me to play with, they thought Glubby would keep me company."

"This is a rather elaborate memory. Did it all return yesterday?"

"It did. The magic mirror must have helped the recollection come back. And when you hear what happened, you'll know why I kept quiet about it."

By this point, I'm leading Grayson on a scenic tour of the city. If we reach Professor Tallon's place too early, I may not get the whole story.

"Glubby was never a healthy fish. If I gave him a magical home, I thought that might fix him. Opal's book said I could build a mirror world by picturing quicksilver magic while thinking about something I *really* wanted. So, I looked at Glubby and thought about him being free. I pictured a fun place for him to live and—POP—he went into his own mirror world. The good part is that he did go into a parallel mini-world… but in Opal's closet."

"Why would that be fun, exactly?"

"It's where Opal kept all her books."

"So Glubby had a lot to read."

"Did I mention I was five?"

"Go on."

"I forgot to picture water in there. I never did get Glubby back."

Pausing, I pull Grayson into my arms. "Let's have a moment of silence."

Grayson leans into my embrace. "Thank you."

When I next speak, I take care to use my most official alpha voice. "We honor your sacrifice, oh Glubby the goldfish."

Grayson giggles again. "Shut up. That was a horrible way for someone to die, even if they are a goldfish."

"I'm a carnivore. The only thing I regret about poor Glubby is that he wasn't seasoned and fried."

"Come on, Glubby was a really sick fish."

"How so?"

"Well, he swam upside down, like all human fish. But he never went very fast."

I pause. "Hey, now. Did Glubby swim or just float around?"

"Come to think of it, he just floated around." Grayson gasps. "Glubby was already dead, wasn't he?"

It's getting harder not to laugh. In some ways, Grayson is mature past her years. In other ways, she thinks dead fish are just swimming upside down.

"Yes, Grayson. Before you sent Glubby into an alternate reality of Opal's closet, your little friend had already swum for that fishbowl in the sky."

"That can't be right. Glubby was from the human world. My parents said all human fish swim upside down."

"I've spent time on Earth. The fish there swim right-side up."

"But I lived in New York, too."

"Which is known for its skyscrapers."

"Okay, you got me there. Lady R never sent me on any errands that involved studying how fish swam in New York Harbor. The closest I got was picking up green milkshakes for her from this juice place by the docks."

"That sounds like Lady R all right."

"I can't believe my parents lied to me."

"In their defense, you were five."

"Hey, I'm half serious about this. Even though I couldn't remember the specifics, some part of me always felt guilty about Glubby."

"I choose to look on the bright side. Somewhere, in a very funny alternate reality, a version of Opal can't understand why her bedroom smells like dead fish. That's a win in my book."

Grayson all-out laughs. "Stop. You'll make me snort."

"That's something I'd like to hear, so—"

I freeze mid-sentence. My inner wolf goes on high alert. My hair stands on end. The insects have fallen silent. Any breeze has died.

Something is wrong.

Not for the first time, I wish I had my sight back.

"We're at the entrance to the city's west end," I state. "Do you see an archway?"

"Yes," replies Grayson. "It has two columns and gargoyles."

"That would be the problem," I state. "Those columns shouldn't have anything atop them. The gargoyles must have been sent here by the Prism Master. He's testing the power of Wulfhelm and me."

I scent brimstone in the air. Grayson is angry. "What. An. Asshat."

"The Prism Master does this often. Last time, he sent stone giants after me." A cool kind of fury overtakes me. Years ago, gargoyles couldn't even dare to fly over Wulfhelm without getting slammed by a column of fire. Now, they'll have to strike the pavement in order to get burned.

I inhale deeper, catching the scent of seaweed and dust. Definitely gargoyles. I don't have the luxury of walking away, even if I wanted to. *Which I most definitely do not.* The Prism Master will interpret my retreat as weakness and send an assassin after more at-risk targets… like the pups.

I start unbuttoning my shirt. Grayson takes a half-step away. "What are you doing?"

"Getting ready for a fight. These are my formal pack leathers. I don't want them to get shredded when I shift."

Somewhere nearby, the gargoyles snicker. Their

voices sound like stones grinding against each other. I picture them in my mind—a pair of tiny humanoids with stone skin and bat wings. They'll have oversized hands, feet and fangs.

And they'll attack as a pair.

GARGOYLES

7

GRAYSON

Two nasty-looking gargoyles eye up Wolf Dex and me. *Can't say I expected this to happen.*

"Have you ever fought gargoyles before?" asks Wolf Dex.

"Ah, no."

"Then, you don't mind if I..." Wolf Dex leaves the logic out there.

"Have at it."

Wolf Dex grins. "Regular human fire will weaken stone. But supernatural flames? Every rock in Wulfhelm is magically treated."

"That's very interesting."

No doubt, Wolf Dex has a greater plan here. I'm too busy having a staring contest with the gargoyles to contemplate what it might be.

Moving as one, the gargoyles leap off their perch and swoop toward us. Wolf Dex hops in front of me, goes down on his front paws and growls. The gargoyles speed toward him. At the last moment, Wolf Dex leaps away. The gargoyles arc back into the air.

Fortunately, the gargoyles don't seem interested in me... yet.

The gargoyles circle around us before making another attack at Wolf Dex. An odd kind of dance follows with the gargoyles winging at Wolf Dex and him avoiding every strike.

Worry corkscrews up my spine. How can Dex fight not one gargoyle, but two? They're made of rock. Even wolf shifters have limits.

Wolf Dex's movements become so fast, his body is a blur. The movements of the gargoyles turn frantic. Wolf Dex makes one last leap. The gargoyles smash into the ground.

Whoosh!

Green flames erupt from the street, encasing the gargoyles in fire. They squawk and flap for a moment, then crumble into dust. Wolf Dex trots back over to me.

"Gargoyles," Wolf Dex proclaims. "Always good for a little exercise."

I set my hand on my throat. "That got my blood pumping."

Wolf Dex nudges my shoulder with his muzzle. "What do you want to do now? Perhaps we should return to Thornfield."

"I'd rather go to Professor Tallon's." Yet, even as I say this, I can't help but wobble from foot to foot.

"Close your eyes."

Of all the things I thought Wolf Dex might say next, that wasn't on the list. After battling two gargoyles, I'm not feeling as sharp as usual. "Why would I close my—"

I never finish my question. Mostly because Dex has changed back into human form. He's now naked and slipping on his black pack leathers. Turns out, the backside view of Dex is just as nice as the front.

Wow. I thought the gargoyle fight was a shocker. I'm no longer wobbling from foot to foot, but now I might have stopped breathing.

Dex finishes changing. Without saying a word, he scoops me into his arms and carries me back to Thornfield.

"I'd tell you to stop, but..." I leave the thought out there.

"But I'm right?"

"That and you're a really good cuddler. Has anyone ever mentioned that to you?"

"No. I don't take that as a critique of my skill." Dex

leans in to whisper in my ear. "You're my first cuddle-ee."

That makes me feel all warm and happy. Dex carries me back to Thornfield. In short order, I change into my nightdress and slip into bed.

From there, you'd think it would be easy to fall asleep. Not so. Wolf Dex is now sitting outside my door as my guardian. It's crazy distracting.

At some point in the night, I give up on the battle to sleep on a mattress. Slipping out of bed, I tiptoe out into the hallway and cuddle with Wolf Dex yet again. This time, Dex's furry body is coiled into a great loop, so I snuggle in at the center.

It's the best night's sleep I can remember.

Thornfield

8

DEX

I awaken to something good and bad.

First, the good. I'm in my wolf form. My body curls onto itself. Grayson sleeps at the center of that circle. Which is beyond good, really.

Second, the bad. The fact that the Prism Master sent gargoyles after me last night means we can't stay here much longer. Grayson and I must find a way to stop the Prism Master and Lady R, fast.

"Owoooooo!"

High-pitched howls echo through the halls, followed by the click-clack of tiny paws speeding across the outer passage. I smile.

The pups are racing through Thornfield again.

Grayson yawns. "Is that what I think it is?"

"Yup. Do you want to join?"

"Absolutely."

I flip over so I lie on the floor. Grayson slips onto my back. Together, we wait.

A chorus of yips sound as fifty pups tear around the corner and come to a skidding stop by me and Grayson.

Wolf Ulliver trots forward. "Will you race with us?"

"Yes," says Grayson. "We'll even give you a ten-second head start."

"Three, two, one, go!" I cry.

The pups take off in a mass. Grayson and I count-down from ten. When we hit zero, we take off around the large corridors.

As always, there's never a particular finish line. The pups just speed around until they eventually miss a turn and end up in the inevitable puppy pile.

Which happens fairly quickly this morning.

The pups are so excited, they miss their first turn and end up in the mother of all puppy piles. When I speak, I try to use my most serious voice as alpha. Trouble is, I'm smiling too hard to pull it off.

"Well done, pack. What else do you plan to do today?"

Wolf Ulliver ambles forward. "We trying something new and *human*." He glances over to Wolf Hiriah as he says the word, *human*. "An obstacle course."

"Oh, my," says Grayson. "That sounds exciting."

Wolf Ulliver puffs up his chest in pride. "We have a climbing wall and everything."

Teacher Clements and the other adults amble around the corner. Like the pups, they're all in their wolf forms.

When I next speak, I press more alpha power into my voice. "Listen to your elders," I tell the pups.

"Yes, Alpha," says Dex. The other pups yip their agreement.

"Now, follow Teacher Clements," I add.

The pups get into neat lines and trot out after their teacher. A band of sorrow tightens across my chest. Normally, Taryn leads the pups. Every member of the pack adds something to the group. Taryn brings a precious mixture of serenity and a dry sense of humor. I miss him.

Once the pups are off, Grayson and I get ready in our casual brown leathers and make our way to Professor Tallon's house. This time, we actually arrive. Although I can't see anything, I know what the place looks like: a three-story clapboard house that's painted black. Grayson and I walk up the steps. Like last time, the door swings open on its own with a long creak.

Grayson and I step inside. "What do you see?" I ask.

"A long hallway. White runes are still scratched on the walls. No paintings are appearing, unlike last time." The tinkling of bells sound. "The mirror is showing up again." Grayson steps closer. "Only, this one has a different frame. It's still silver and a portal, but there's green energy in it, too. It's connected to somewhere in the present."

A weight of worry seeps from my shoulders. "Are you thinking what I am?"

"Yes," says Grayson. "If worse comes to worst, we can use this to evacuate the pack."

"That's good, so why do I scent worry coming from you?"

"It's just too perfect. I wonder if it's… you know…"

"A trap," I finish. "Good point." Stepping forward, I rest my hand on the base of Grayson's back. "So far, you've seen the spells and magic of Professor Coffindoffer. He was the last Rune Druid and quite the jokester. The library is another matter. It's the sacred room of our greatest Rune Druid, Professor Tallon. If anyone worked with Xao and Ishir on the ritual to recharge Wulfhelm, it would be Tallon."

"Can't wait," says Grayson.

Like the city outside, the interior of the Rune Druid's house is also well-known territory for me. I guide Grayson to a large door that's covered in more chalk symbols. Grayson pulls on the handle to reveal a very different space inside.

We enter a traditional library with wooden shelves

that are packed with leather-bound books. A large painting adorns one wall. It shows the room, only with Professor Tallon standing by his favorite reading chair.

"Well?" I ask.

"Wow," says Grayson. "Professor Tallon is a total badass."

PROFESSOR
TALLON

9

GRAYSON

Dex and I settle into the library. Hours pass as we check through the place. I focus on the book while Dex takes the professor's desk.

I quickly find the books Hiriah and the other girl pups read—the book covers are dotted in muddy paw prints. These volumes outline the basics of osmos magic. Looking further, I discover volumes on river naiad power that—since it leverages reflections on water—isn't that different from osmos magic.

Professor Tallon writes in the margins of everything. There are even a few notes that mention Elise.

How would Master Tallon have known my harpy friend?

I turn the idea around for a few minutes before deciding that everyone seems to know Elise. She's one of those fae.

"Oh, I've got a good one," I announce.

Dex still sits at the professor's desk. Since the drawers are packed with especially magical stuff, Dex can easily see almost everything there. For the past few minutes, he's been prying at the back of a drawer, looking for yet another hidden compartment.

"Let's hear it," says Dex.

I clear my throat as I read from a particularly juicy margin note. "The professor writes, *this pointy-nosed fool shouldn't pontificate about river naiads.*"

Dex laughs. "That is his best one yet."

"No one insults better than Professor Tallon."

The section that Dex had been working on now breaks free. With careful movements, Dex sets a long drawer onto the desktop. It's one of the few times it's obvious that Dex cannot see.

The back of the drawer pops open. Dex gingerly pulls out a small wooden box. "Now, this I can see perfectly. It's loaded with magic." He runs his fingertips across the cover. "There's a message carved in the wood. It reads, *For the day Ishir, Xao and Tallon unlock the secrets for the ceremony to recharge Wulfhelm.*"

That gets my attention. Rising, I move to stand by Dex's shoulder. My pulse speeds as Dex carefully pries the wooden box open. When he next speaks, his voice is low with awe.

"Wow."

I lean in for a better look. "What is it?"

"Beef jerky." Dex inhales deeply. "There's magic on it to enhance the flavor. I haven't seen anything like this since I was a kid."

"There's a note on top."

Dex pats the box until he finds the small scrap of paper. He hands me the message. "What does it say?"

I unfold the sheet and read aloud. "*Enjoy these after Wulfhelm is healed. In case of emergency, I've recorded the results of every test we conducted over the last twenty years. My journal is stored in the attic along with more delicacies. Best, Professor Tallon.*"

Dex arches his right brow. "Twenty years? They were at this far longer than I thought."

I slump. "How sad that they never finished the ritual and got to enjoy their reward."

"It's sad…ish. You've no idea how good this stuff is." Dex pats the box and pulls out a thin strip of dried meat. "You have to try some."

"At the Bartlebee, I lived on the same meal three times a day. It's been a big deal for me to expand my cuisine into cheese sandwiches. Maybe later."

With shifter speed, Dex scoops me onto his lap. He takes a bite of the beef jerky before gently brushing his lips across mine. The kiss is delicate and toe-curlingly good. And it leaves behind the hint of a rich and gamey flavor.

"I take it back," I state. "I'll try some."

We spend the next ten minutes trading bites and kisses. Once the box is empty, Dex announces that he'll find the rest of the treat in the attic, reasoning that although he can't see, his sense of wolf-smell will lead him in the right direction.

I decide that it's best not to get between a werewolf and his beef jerky.

"Have fun," I call as Dex leaves the library.

I settle back into Professor Tallon's favorite chair. Flipping open a nearby book, I go back to reading about river naiads.

Pop, pop, pop!

A familiar sound echoes through the room. Once again, a magic mirror appears on a nearby wall. That part isn't so shocking. This seems to be happening a lot to me lately.

Rising, I cross the room and check out the mirror's reflection. A jolt of alarm moves through my nervous system.

Lady R is in the mirror.

She looks unchanged from when I last saw her in

New York. She's still elf-perfect with even features and an icy stare.

Lady R smiles, but there's nothing but loathing behind her grin. She speaks two words with relish.

"Hello, sister."

LADY RAPUNZEL

GRAYSON

The words still echo in my mind.

Hello, sister.

This is really happening.

"Speechless?" asks Lady R. "Can't guess where I am, can you?"

"You're in the reception room of the Prism Master's palace. It holds some powerful mirrors. You activated one of them."

"And how would you know the Prism Master's palace?" Lady R looks around, as if trying to find the answer in the room. "Ah, that's right. You fell through the ceiling."

"Correct," I state. "When I escaped the Bartlebee."

Lady R leans forward, her eyes bright. As her tower tithe, I learned to read Lady R's moods. That's how I know what this particular expression means: Lady R is fishing for information.

"Who cast that pendant around your neck? Because we both know it isn't you."

"Then why ask?" The answer appears. "Because you were told to do it. The Prism Master is curious about my skills. You're not."

"Because I know you're incapable of any serious magic. If you knew how you cast that pendant, you certainly would have told me. Which means that pendant spell is something someone did for you. Was it the harpy, Elise?"

I frown. "How could Elise manage that?"

"You're a horrible liar. Of course, it's the harpy."

"If there's nothing else, I'll get back to reading—" I almost call her Lady R, but decide to use her other name. "—Opal."

"How do you know that name? You remember nothing from our childhood. Did the harpy do a favor for you?"

"You tell me. You're the next quintessence."

"Exactly!" Lady R's face reddens with rage. "This is all leading to my reign. You think you have the power of the Osmos Queen, but you're wrong. You're merely a sheep with a magical fleece that's mine to skin. I'm the one who'll ultimately succeed. You've no idea how deep this all goes… and the power that's really on my side."

I'm not ready to consider if I'm the next Osmos Queen, but it's good to know Lady R still wants the crown.

I should ask something else. I tap my lip and try to recall. There was something in the mirror with Xao that's important. Only in all the excitement, I can't remember what it was. A flower of some kind? I can almost grasp the memory, but not quite.

"I won't prolong this little family disaster," says Lady R. "All I'll say is that your precious Wulfhelm is surrounded. You've forty-eight hours before the so-called fires of Wulfhelm are low enough for the Prism Master's warriors to invade. And once they're all in?" She smirks. "Oh, what delights await you and your pups."

I know the floor doesn't really drop out from under me, but it certainly feels that way. Just hours ago, Dex and I were racing the pups through the halls of Thornfield. It's not possible that our world has forty-eight more hours to exist.

My eyes sting with grief and fear. *This can't be happening.*

"Oh, look." Lady R chuckles. "She's about to cry.

Well, I'm doing you a favor by being cruel. You've no confidence in your mate. You've no confidence in yourself. And you've no idea what it truly means to recharge the magic of Wulfhelm. You don't have a killer instinct. That's what it takes to succeed in the Faerie Realm."

I open my mouth, ready to say something. No words come out.

Lady R leans in closer. "The Prism Master vows that I may live in Thornfield once you're gone. That way, Dex doesn't have to even change his bed, just make room for me in it."

A sickly feeling crawls up my throat. Again, I wish for some perfect retort. Nothing comes.

Pop, pop, pop!

The mirror vanishes. I don't know how long I stare at the spot where the mirror just appeared. My legs turn watery. I picture the pups racing through Thornfield while yipping with joy.

There simply must be some way to save them.

11

DEX

*L*eaving Grayson behind, I make my way through the maze of hallways that make up the rest of the house. Unlike Professor Tallon's well-organized library, the remainder of the building is classic Rune Druid.

Which is to say, nutty.

Doorways open to brick walls. Passages magically loop on themselves before leading to staircases that go up and down at the same time. I know why the pups snuck in here. It's a lot of fun unless you want to find a hard-to-find spot.

Fortunately, I have a new scent to follow. *Magical beef jerky.* At last, I catch that delicious smell. Following it, I reach a lone chain hanging from the rafters. I pull the line; a set of stairs arc down from the ceiling.

Climbing up the rickety steps, I enter the attic itself. I'd hoped some stuff here would be magical. That way, I wouldn't be in pure darkness.

No such luck.

I inspect the room by hand, moving from left to right. The place is a collection of boxes, clothes and knick-knacks. There are even a few human weapons tossed into the mix. I'm halfway around when I find another hand-carved container that glows with magic. The words on top read, *Wulfhelm Experiments.*

Opening the box, I find two delights. The first is another packet with beef jerky. The second is a pile of parchments that are sewn together along one side. *A homemade book.* I flip through the volume. The pages are covered in scribblings by Professor Tallon. His ink must have some magic, since it glows yellow to my eyes.

After being unable to see for so long, my pulse speeds at the idea of reading something new. I start at page one.

In this journal, I, Professor Tallon, shall record my experiments to recharge the magic of Wulfhelm.

Year One

I ask Ishir and Xao to hold hands while touching the Muster Tree. Since this arbor contains the failsafe for turning off the fires of Wulfhelm, it should be the best place to recharge them as well. This is unsuccessful.

Year Two
After many tries by the Muster Tree, I ask other shifters to stand nearby during the ceremony. This seems to help as they can contribute their magic. It's still not enough, though.

Year Three
We've moved the ritual site from the Muster Tree onto osmos land. This gives a better result, although it's still not working. Unfortunately, everyone in the ceremony must move to osmos territory so they can join ongoing tests. Most of our strongest shifters are now in osmos. The remaining adults shifters are leaving Wulfhelm in droves. Still, we must persevere!

I flip forward to a dog-eared page at the back of the journal.

Year Twenty Three
Still no Alpha for Wulfhelm. Only a handful of adult teachers remain with the orphans. But it's all been worth it—we finally have a breakthrough! I've found the right group of powerful shifters and osmos magic users to join Ishir and Xao during the ceremony. Even better, we've discovered the right places for everyone to stand. This will work! The final test takes

place in two weeks. I shall send this journal back to Wulfhelm for safekeeping, just in case. It's almost done!

From here, I know the story. The ritual was sabotaged. Everyone died. Another Alpha, Wyatt, could have taken over Wulfhelm... Only Wyatt disappeared. Taryn showed me some pictures of Wyatt, but I think they're fake. I doubt Wyatt ever got close to Wulfhelm. No question why, either. Wyatt was refused by his fated mate, who was none other than Opal. She refused him, becaming a Rapunzel instead. Wyatt probably died of a broken heart. This kind of thing is rare, but it happens.

Here's where I come into the story. My father had abandoned me when I was kid. Taryn found me in the woods and brought me to Wulfhelm. I've been Alpha ever since.

I rescan the pages. My instincts tell me that something about the ritual and Taryn form a larger realization. The big picture is almost there, but it stays just out of my line of vision.

Pop, pop, pop!

By now, I know this sound. A mirror is about to appear. I expect it to materialize on the wall.

That doesn't happen.

This time, the mirror appears below my feet. Fast as a heartbeat, it turns from a solid reflection into liquid silver. My boots sink into the gooey mirror. I try to run, but it's no use.

I fall through the floor.

Perfect darkness surrounds me. I tumble through empty space until I land in a new spot that's not Professor Tallon's attic. Instead, I stand on a familiar stretch of beach. The place is all muddy sand, churning seas and an old rusted tower.

It's the estuary, my childhood home.

My family are vassals to the Fortitude elves, a group of fae who wield the power of huge magical creatures. In my family, we care for mega beasts of the seagoing variety. I even kept a pet Kraken.

For a moment, I wonder if my friend, Prince Jacoby, has drawn me here. We used to play in this ocean.

Silver mist appears nearby. *Magic.* A new figure materializes: a man who combines the best of elf perfection with the worst of its malice.

The Prism Master.

PRISM MASTER

12

DEX

"Greetings, Dex." The Prism Master gestures across the beach. "How do you like visiting your old home? I ordered this mirror to transport you to the past."

"You shouldn't have done that. It's never a good idea to order mirrors around."

The Prism Master lifts his chin. "That's a myth."

"We live in the land of myths. And you have a castleful of stolen mirrors from Queen Xao. You rarely use them. That *was* wise." I take care to emphasize the word *was*.

The Prism Master's mouth thins to an angry line. He points in the opposite direction. "See that small figure? Brown leathers, blue skin and scales?"

My heart sinks. There's only one person who meets that description. My father, Shoal.

Sure enough, my father marches across a far-off stretch of beach while untangling nets. The sight is like a punch to my abdomen. Shoal hated me. And he loved visiting the Prism Master and drinking enchanted wine. If I hadn't met Jacoby, I don't know how I could have stayed sane.

"Oh, how your father loathed you," says the Prism Master. "He'd tell me over a flagon of wine: *how can a man of the oceans sire a rodent?*"

It takes an effort, but I keep my features calm. "I recall what my father said."

"He thought you clawed your way out of your mother's womb. That's why she died in childbirth."

Deep in my soul, my wolf growls with rage. The Prism Master is trying to start a fight and my inner animal wants to give him one. However, my human side knows that if the Prism Master wants something, then it's best to deny him.

I make a point of meeting the Prism Master's gaze. "Other than attempting to anger me, why are you here now? Want some pointers on how to fight gargoyles?"

"Don't you ever wonder why I hate you so much?"

"You've destroyed your own land, Refraction. You want Wulfhelm. The rest is a lot of show."

The Prism Master chuckles. "I brought you here today in order to discover if you're still a fool. Fortunately, you are." He steps closer. "Even after all these years, you've no idea who I really am and what I want."

"You think that's some secret? I know you want Wulfhelm. My father came to your lands seeking a wish from one of your mirrors. Shoal wanted to take the wolf out of me. And you took the opportunity to destroy him because I might be Alpha one day."

For a moment, it's like I'm back in the attic and looking over Professor Tallon's journal.

There's a bigger realization here. I'm missing it.

"I did not destroy Shoal for Wulfhelm. And your land is not why I'll ruin you."

"You're trying to bait my wolf again," I state. "It won't work. I'll ask you again. What do you want?"

"Why, to give you a chance, of course. Soon the fires will be low enough—and my new armor strong enough —to allow my warriors onto Wulfhelm land." He lowers his voice. "Once we're on your territory, I know how to shut down your protective fires. All I need to do is cut down the Muster Tree."

It's an effort not to gasp. Indeed, that will turn off the fires Wulfhelm. But it's something the pack leaders never discuss.

"Don't bother trying to recharge the ground," says

the Prism Master. "Ishir and Xao couldn't do it, and they had dozens of osmos and shifters to boost their powers. You have no chance."

As the Prism Master speaks these words, he watches me closely. It's another test. He wants to see if I'll reveal whether Grayson is strong enough to recharge Wulfhelm.

"Don't you think it's hopeless? Tell me. Say the words: Grayson doesn't have enough magic to save my pack."

Talking with the Prism Master is always a verbal battle. This is the latest volley. No doubt, Lady R has told the Prism Master that her sister, Grayson, is useless.

"No," I counter. "You tell me. You were the one who trapped Grayson in the Bartlebee for years, just to see if she had the magic to escape."

The Prism Master purses his lips. "You have until midnight tomorrow to evacuate."

"And this is why you've brought me here?"

"Of course." The Prism Master smiles. "I'm not heartless. After the battle with the gargoyles, I know you'd suspect my attack. I wanted to put your mind at rest and give you time to move the pups to safety."

After years of verbal sparring, I know what this so-called warning really means. The Prism Master isn't waiting until tomorrow to attack. We're probably surrounded.

He'll attack tonight.

Pop, pop!

The familiar sounds echo along the beach. The sand beneath my feet takes on the look of quicksilver. I fall through the ground again.

Moments later, I land in the attic with one thought on my mind.

I must find Grayson.

13

GRAYSON

Not sure how long I sit in the wooden chair by the library window. At some point, Dex strides back into the room and pauses.

"I scent your fear and anger," he says simply.

"Lady R appeared to me in a mirror."

Dex isn't the only one who can scent a change in the air. The tang of sweat and vinegar—that's worry and rage—fills my senses. The truth appears in my mind. Lady R contacted me with mirrors from the Prism Master. And I know my old jailer. He'd never allow Lady R to rifle through his precious collection alone.

Which means the Prism Master was using mirrors, too.

I rush over to Dex. "The Prism Master opened a mirror to you in the attic."

Dex nods. "He says he'll attack tomorrow at midnight."

A jolt of alarm runs down my back. "The Prism Master is trying to lull us into a false sense of safety. He could invade any time now." Closing my eyes, I pull on the swirl of magic inside me, focusing the power to my hands. Nothing happens.

"I can see your body glow with emerald power," says Dex. "What's happening?"

"I'm trying to cast a mirror and see what the Prism Master is up to." I push more magic through my limbs. A few green sparks light up over my palms. "It's not working."

In fact, quite the opposite is the case. Every nerve ending in my body burns with pain as the spell fails. I hiss in a breath before releasing my magic. "Damn."

Dex pulls me against him. "Don't hurt yourself. It's standard practice to shut off communications before you invade. The Prism Master is using his mirrors from Queen Xao to block your magic."

"Maybe I can't use my power," I agree. "But what if something else can? Earlier today, we saw that mirror in the hallway."

"Good thinking."

Dex and I rush out to the spot. "This mirror still

active," exclaims Dex. "The Prism Master hasn't blocked it. I can see green magic inside the frame."

"Same here." I tap my cheek and think things through. "It looks as if this is opening a passage to someplace in our present."

Dex focuses on the white haze inside the mirror's inner reflection. When he speaks again, his voice is low and confident. "Help us."

Bit by bit, the mirror's interior comes into focus. An image appears—it's a small cottage surrounded by wide rolling hills. "This is working." A jolt of happy moves through my nervous system. "The mirror is showing us someplace in Faerie."

"You know how I have my cabin? This is the cottage of my friend, Jacoby."

"As in, Prince Jacoby?"

"Yes, do you know him?"

"Elise used to talk about him. She's a great admirer of Prince Jacoby's mighty horde of battle beasts." I stare at the image in the mirror. "His home is deserted. It's perfect for the pups to hide out, if we need to evacuate Wulfhelm. Is there a good place to check if the Prism Master's army is really about to invade?"

Dex rubs his neck. "There's a cliff along the Wulfhelm border with Refraction. It's the best place to check the

Prism Master's land without being seen." Dex sets his hands on my shoulders. His touch is warm and centering. "I still scent your pain. What else did Lady R say?"

"Things to upset me. It's nothing we should worry about now. What about you?"

"The Prism Master did the same, only…"

I tilt my head. "What is it?"

"There's something I'm still not seeing about the Prism Master. I need more time to think." He sighs. "That will have to wait for later, though."

I nod. "We better go."

Dex and I speed toward the door. The moment we hit the threshold, Dex's body erupts into his wolf form. I leap onto his back as Wolf Dex races toward the border between Refraction and Wulfhelm.

As we run through the forest, I sort through all the ways this could be some trick from the Prism Master. It wouldn't be the first time he tried to fool me about something.

Yet, even as I try to console myself that the worst *isn't* about to happen, part of me knows the truth. The Prism Master and Lady R have been plotting to end me, Dex and Wulfhelm for years.

And their killing blow is about to land.

14

DEX

I race through the forest in my wolf form. Alpha energy churns through me, driving my body to go faster than ever before. Grayson and I soon reach the lookout point between Wulfhelm and Refraction. Although I remain blinded, I can picture the spot easily enough: it's a tall outcrop of rock that's flat on one side.

Lying down, I catch my breath. Since I'm in my wolf form, this involves a lot of panting. Grayson slides off y back.

"Crawl up to the peak on your stomach," I urge. "Check over the top edge. Tell me what you see."

"Got it." Rustling sounds follow as Grayson makes her way to the lookout point.

Her scent takes on the edge of salt and copper. It's

the most intense mixture of fear and pain that I can ever recall from my vita. All of which is why I know what Grayson will report to me even before she returns.

"The plains of Refraction are overrun," reports Grayson. "There are soldiers in silver armor everywhere."

"Those are refract warriors," I state. "They're the Prism Master's army. Did you see anyone else?"

"I spotted other fighters in plague masks and elf warriors on horseback. There are also trolls with clubs." She lowers her voice. "And I spied a whole herd of minotaurs."

It's one thing to expect a betrayal. It's another to be faced with the fact. "That's Jacoby. He's joined the Prism Master."

"I'm sorry."

I force my demeanor to stay calm. "He warned me about this. Jacoby must follow the dictates of his brother, the king." Still, I can't help but feel the blood drain from my body. I've seen Jacoby's battle herd. This won't end well. "Who else was there? Anyone with wings? More gargoyles?"

"There are only harpies." Grayson tries to keep her voice stable, but there's no mistaking the misery in her tone. "Elise won't let her legions share the skies with other winged warriors. She says they only get in her way." Grayson runs her fingertips over the fur on my front paw. "This is bad."

"Not entirely," I say. "The armies aren't yet on Wulfhelm lands. That means the fires are still too powerful for them to cross over. Were you able to get a good look at their armor?"

"No, the refract warriors were too far away."

"The Prism Master claimed his fighters could march onto Wulfhelm land and tear down the Muster Tree, leaving us helpless. I need to get a better look at their armor."

"I did see something."

"What?"

"There are some ruins along the border. I caught the glimpse of what could be armor, but my eyes might be playing tricks on me. That's Wulfhelm territory. Any enemy warriors shouldn't be able to cross over."

"They could if they have good intentions."

"You're thinking about Captain Zoya."

"She's been a good ally, so far as she's able. Once the Prism Master stole her father's throne, Zoya had to serve him." I close my eyes, picturing the fastest path to the ruins. "I know just how to get there."

Grayson climbs on my back once more. "Let's go."

This time, I take a slower pace. The best path to the ruins goes through a lot of very sharp rocks. It takes a while, but we soon reach what remains of an old border fort.

Sure enough, Zoya is there.

Sadly, her armor is laden with so much magic, even I can see it.

ZOYA

15

DEX

For a moment, it's all I can do to stare. Thanks to my blindness spell, Zoya looks like an enchanted suit of silver armor that exists in a world of total darkness.

"Last time I came to Wulfhelm, the fires burned me," says Zoya. "That's because I was in your lands for the Prism Master. His ill intent set off the protective flames. Now, I come here because I wish to help." She re-sheathes her sword. "I hope the lack of fire proves my intent."

"It does," I state.

"Is this your vita?" asks Zoya.

Grayson moves to stand at my side. "I am."

Even though this is a terrible situation, I feel a swell of pride at hearing these words from Grayson.

"You never knew my father," says Zoya. "He was a true partner to the osmos quintessence. Queen Xao would create mirrors that would appear in the great crystal dome. My father would decide who deserved what wishes."

"Everyone has heard of your father," I state. "He was a true king."

"I saw the Refract armies," offers Grayson.

"You're surrounded on all sides," says Zoya. "Armies cover on the plain. Harpies own the sky. Mole rats and other creatures patrol below ground. There is no way to escape."

I've dreaded this moment for so long. *Wulfhelm is about to be invaded.* Now that it's here, there's a sense of determination. *Grayson and I won't allow this to happen.*

"How long do we have?" I ask.

"Three o'clock in the morning," answers Zoya. "The Prism Master figures everyone will be asleep by then."

Speaking of the Prism Master, his voice echoes in from a distance. "Captain Zoya? Where are you?"

"You better go," says Grayson. "The Prism Master isn't a patient guy."

Zoya nods. "Best of luck to you and yours. If anyone can find a way out of this, it's the two of you." Zoya steps off into the ruin. The light from her armor vanishes. Soon, I'm back to seeing nothing at all.

"Maybe we should escape through the mirror," I offer. "And save who we can along the way. Perhaps your prophecy is right. Once we leave, maybe a wish on the right mirror can put everything right again."

Grayson is silent for a long time. All I scent from her is rage. "I've spent my life being bossed around by Lady R and the Prism Master. We have instructions from Professor Tallon. Maybe we can recharge the power of Wulfhelm at the Muster Tree. I don't know about you, but I can't give up without trying." Her voice takes on the hint of a growl. "If they set foot on our lands with dark intent, I want them to burn and run."

Warmth and confidence flow through me. *This is what it means to find your fated mate.* We boost each other.

"I'd like to see that, too." I lie down on the rocky ground. Grayson crawls onto my wolf-back and together, we race back to pack lands.

At long last, it's time to try and recharge the magic of Wulfhelm.

16

GRAYSON

By the time we return to Wulfhelm, it's almost midnight. After talking with the teachers, we decide it's best to evacuate the pups to safety. We bring in the mirror from the Rune Druid's house and set it up inside Thornfield.

Next, we wake up the pups. They're still trying to out-human each other, so the pack is sleeping in Thornfield. The pups are in human form and dress, along with their teachers. We gather them before Professor Tallon's mirror.

Then, it's time to say good-bye.

Watching the pups step through the mirror, it feels as if my heart's being torn from my chest. They're all so trusting and innocent. To them, this is all a big game.

My six students are last through the mirror portal. It takes everything in me not to run after them.

After all, Dex and I are only making educated guesses. Who knows if this ceremony will work? One part of my soul—my inner fae—says I should escape with the pups. But that's not in control now. My troll heritage is running the show. That part of me wants to protect my mate and territory.

With the pups and teachers gone, Dex and I head for the Muster Tree. Both of us are in human form and wearing pack leathers.

Dex kneels before the arbor. "Before we start, I should test the ground."

It takes a moment before I realize what Dex is talking about. "Oh, you want to check the power of Wulfhelm."

"Right."

Dex curls his fingers into the soft grass. Green, waist-high flames flare up from the ground. Since it's magic, Dex can see the fire. Based on how the lines on his face tighten, he isn't happy with what he sees.

"As Alpha of the Wulfhelm pack, I ask the fires to reveal their secrets to me. What's the risk to Wulfhelm?" Some green sparks kick up, but there's no vision of the Prism Master's plans. Dex shakes his head. "I didn't expect it to work. The Prism Master's blocking spell is still in place. Still, it was worth a try."

An odd scent carries on the air. I don't know who it is, but it's definitely the smell of strangers. "We should get started."

"Right. Based on Professor Tallon's notes, you and I must stand face-to-face with one hand touching the tree's bark."

We get into position. I feel the rough bark of the Muster Tree under my palm. "All set," I announce.

"Professor Tallon's notes said we must picture the quicksilver magic and focus on what we want."

I shake my head. "Wow, that's exactly what happened when I cast the spell for my gold—" I bite my lips together.

"Hey, I still consider your Glubby spell to be a big success. Now, we just need to do it again. Together."

Again, Dex has that power to somehow make everything not only fine, but a little lighthearted. Taking a deep breath, I picture the quicksilver of osmos magic while wishing for the grounds of Wulfhelm to be strong once more.

A silver haze of magic appears above my hand. The same happens to Dex. A spark of hope ignites in my soul.

Dex grins. "This may be working."

Silver magic crawls up the tree trunk. Within seconds, the arbor transforms from wood into something that looks like metal. White light dances within the swirling silver.

"This isn't how it worked Xao and Ishir," I state. "It must be related to how you're alpha of the pack."

"No," says Dex gently. "It's because you're the strongest quintessence in the history of Faerie."

His words hang in the air between us. Maybe Lady R and the Prism Master are wrong. Perhaps I do have real power, after all.

Suddenly, the entire tree erupts in silver light. Green flames ignite all around us. Like always, they warm but do not burn. The fire whips toward Dex.

Then the flames go inside him.

Emerald light and fire burns within Dex. Brightness emanates out of his pores. I'm torn between worrying about my mate and staring in awe at the sight before me. While my osmos magic charges the tree, the power of Wulfhelm goes into Dex. He closes his eyes.

Long seconds tick by. "Are you alright?"

Dex opens his eyes. For the first time in what feels like ever, he looks right at me.

"I can see."

And that's when everything goes haywire.

DEX

A wall of refract warriors speed out from the tree line, covering the ground in a new kind of silver. Green flame erupts everywhere, but it doesn't stop the fighters. While the rest of the army goes into position, six soldiers race for the Muster Tree. Their heavy axes gleam in the moonlight. A jolt of alarm moves through my limbs.

Oh, no. They'll cut down the Muster Tree and end the power of Wulfhelm.

It all happens so fast, there's barely time to catch what's happening, let alone act. The warriors swing their axes in a precise rhythm, quickly chopping a wedge into the arbor's trunk. The silver magic fades. What was once metallic wood becomes regular bark again.

With an ear-splitting boom, the Muster Tree careens to the ground. Despair and shock churn through me in equal measure.

With the tree dead, the flames of Wulfhelm retreat into earth.

The Prism Master steps forward. "There, your little campfire is over."

As if in reply, a great column of green flame erupts once more. Only this time, the fire surrounds me in a great column. Although it doesn't burn, I feel power seep through every cell in my body. My veins pop. My bone marrow vibrates with energy. The pillar of green flame swirls around me before zooming into the night sky. A play of emerald light dances through the night clouds.

Then it's gone.

The fires of Wulfhelm are no more.

"What was that?" asks the Prism Master.

I have no idea why that happened, but there's no way I'm telling the Prism Master any of that. Instead, I settle on asking a question.

"If I knew, would I tell you?"

"I don't suppose you'd be smart enough to know how that spell works." The Prism Master snaps his fingers.

Even more troops march out from the woods. I count summer and winter elves as well as ogres and trolls. Even Jacoby is there with his minotaur warriors. Overhead, harpies take to the skies. All of them are in their human form, complete with armor. As the many flying warriors soar past the moon, the scene becomes cast in shifting beams of light.

On the ground, the many warriors march into preset positions, creating concentric circles around me and Grayson. All of them point their swords, spears or arrows in our direction.

My mind races through options. There aren't many.

Grayson steps closer. "We have one surprise left," she whispers.

And that's all Grayson needs to say. I know exactly what she means.

No one here knows I have my sight back.

I pull her against my side. When I next speak, it's in a tone only she can hear. "Be ready to ride."

Grayson nods. From the point of view of the many warriors all around, my mate looks casual and confident. If I weren't holding her so closely, I wouldn't know she was shaking.

"Make way!" cries the Prism Master.

The warrior steps aside, creating an aisle through the crowd. The Prism Master marches even closer. He wears an overblown version of the refract warrior armor, complete with an oversized shield. I'd laugh if I wasn't certain I'd lose my head. After all, the axe-wielding warriors remain only a few feet away.

"I designed this armor myself," says the Prism Master. "Don't you like it?"

"It's very *you*," says Grayson.

The Prism Master sniffs. "You never did know when to shut up." He lifts his shield. "This may appear to be a standard part of refract warrior armor, but I have improved it." The Prism Master flips the shield around, showing that the interior is actually a mirror.

"That's the *Tzar's Ire*," whispers Grayson. "It's a famous mirror that administers poison."

"You know your magic mirrors." The Prism Master angles the shield so we can clearly see the reflection.

It's an effort not to scream.

Inside the Prism Master's shield, there's the image of Jacoby's cottage and all the pups.

My blood chills. *He's going to poison them all.*

"Don't do this," I plead. "The pups have nothing to do with us."

"Yes," adds Grayson. "Dex and I will do anything. Let them live."

The Prism Master sneers. "If I leave them alive, they'll only avenge you. I know how shifters think."

The Prism Master's words rattle through my mind. *I*

know how shifters think. That means something. But what?

Before I can puzzle out the greater pattern, the Prism Whispers to his mirror. "I wish you'd poison all the Wulfhelm shifters who ran away."

Inside the mirror's reflection, black mist fills the air around Jacoby's cottage. Some of the children cough. Others scream in terror. More double over in pain.

My heart cracks.

But my vita growls.

18

GRAYSON

White hot rage courses through me. My students. My pups.

It's a reflex to reach toward the Prism Master's shield. "You bastard! How dare you hurt them?"

That fae side of my soul seems to float outside of my body, looking down upon this scene as if from a great height. I watch myself scream with rage while a silver mist forms over my palms.

"No!" I cry. "Leave them alone!"

The metallic haze over my hands turns into liquid ribbons of silver that whip toward the Prism Master's mirror-shield. The shield's reflective surface turns liquid as my lines of power burrow inside the mirror itself. From my perch up above, I watch with calm disinterest as the Prism Master's face reddens with fury.

"Lady R warned me about you!" cries the Prism Master. "This is another one of your tricks!"

What happens next seems to take forever. In reality, only a few seconds pass as the ribbons of silver power whip back out of the mirror-shield.

And they burrow into my chest.

A shock of energy and magic snaps me out of my reverie. I'm no longer two people, one who watches and the other who casts spells. I'm back to being one Grayson, albeit one who's probably getting skewered by my own magic.

That's not what's actually happening, though.

The power of the silver magic isn't going into me, it's entering the pendant that holds Taryn and Jocasta. I blink once. Twice.

This can't be real.

The silver light goes out. Now, my mirror pendant contains Taryn, Jocasta, and every other shifter from Wulfhelm.

A charged kind of quiet takes over the clearing. All the warriors stare in silence. The questions are out there, even if none of them are asked aloud.

Will she attack us next?

Should we advance or retreat?

And who is this little elf-troll?

While multiple armies stare on in awe, Dex goes into

action. Summoning his inner shifter magic, he transforms into his wolf shape. I'm too stunned to move, so Wolf Dex nips the back of my leather jacket in his massive jaws. With a flick of his head, he tosses me onto his back.

At this point, it's muscle memory for me to lean in and grab onto his fur.

Wolf Dex takes off at a run.

And since Wolf Dex can now see, he chooses a strategic path: right toward Jacoby's army of minotaurs.

Sure, Dex trusts Jacoby with his life. But right now, the prince looks fierce in his silver armor. With so many watching, I can't imagine he'll do anything but kill us.

Even so, if Wolf Dex moves fast enough, perhaps Jacoby may not have a chance to strike.

JACOBY

19

DEX

I speed toward Jacoby in a zig-zag pattern. Fortunately, all the warriors are still shocked and waiting for orders. I leap toward a particularly large orc, using his broad back as a springboard to leap over a cluster of winter elves. Some winter fae grab ice arrows from their quivers and aim for me and Grayson. Still, their movements are sluggish and unsure.

Jacoby stands in a pool of moonlight. He looks as if he's ready to slice me open. Even so, I've seen that look on Jacoby before. He can't seriously plan to kill me and my mate… right?

As I close in, I'm starting to question my friend's loyalty when it happens.

Jacoby winks.

Screeches echo down from the sky. Shadows crawl

across the ground. A fresh jolt of adrenaline moves through me as a legion of harpies swoop in. Elise flies at the front of the group.

Please, let Elise and Jacoby be working together.

"This prey is ours!" shouts Elise.

The harpies fly in a beeline toward Jacoby. My friend watches them but doesn't flinch. Still, he does call out to his minotaur troops.

"Stand down!" calls Jacoby.

The minotaurs go down on one knee. I dodge around these mighty warriors. A few make a half-hearted attempt to crush me or Grayson with their war hammers. It isn't clear if they're only pretending to attack... or if I'm racing too quickly for them to act.

Perhaps it's a little bit of both.

As Grayson and I speed through the minotaur army, the harpies swoop overhead. Like the minotaurs, some stab at us with their weapons. Again, the strikes are too weak to really connect.

I push myself to race faster. At last, I break past the main army and into the pack lands beyond. In the distance, I hear the Prism Master screaming. "Catch them!"

I'm vaguely aware of the harpies circling back toward the destroyed Muster Tree... and the Prism

Master. If this were a regular day, I might wonder what she's doing.

But this day is anything but typical. I focus on running.

My family kept a cave by the beach by the Estuary. No one knows about it—not even my father or the Prism Master. I speed along toward my homeland. At some point, I'm aware that no one's following me and Grayson. There are no foreign scents on the air, either.

They aren't tracking us. *How long can that last?*

Finally, I reach the beach. The moon reflects off the churning surf. A rock wall rises from the sand. The entrance to my secret cave opens up on the base of the stone barrier. I take a few cautious steps inside. The place smells stale, but there's no trace of anyone entering my old hiding spot. I collapse onto my stomach and pant for breath. Grayson slides off my back. Without saying a word, she sorts through my old supplies, bringing out a canteen of water and pouring it on my tongue.

As I drink, I stare out the cave's entrance. For a moment, I think I see Elise darkening the sky. The image it's gone too quickly to be sure, though.

I finish gulping my water, then collapse into an uneasy sleep.

Elise

20

GRAYSON

For a long while, it's all I can do to watch Wolf Dex sleep. Then, my old habits with lupines come back to me in a rush. To heal, I set my hands on the animal. My inner magic then moves into the wolf's body. A mental picture will soon appear, showing me what must be healed.

Kneeling beside the sleeping Dex, I set my hands onto his soft fur. I close my eyes and try to tap my inner magic. Normally, there's a constant swirl of it inside me.

Only when I close my eyes this time, I find no green magic within. There's a chilly swirl of silver power. Some heat from red energy. But there's nothing like the familiar green whirlpool of healing power.

I turn this change over in my mind. Dex was connected to the Muster Tree when the power of

Wulfhelm went into him. And since I was touching the trunk, I was part of that loop as well.

Could Dex have taken in my green magic as well as Wulfhelm's?

To test this out, I revert to an old-fashioned way of healing: searching Dex's fur for any breaks or cuts. A hefty slice marks his front leg. The wound is deep—probably from a long sword. It's the kind of injury that takes me a few minutes to heal.

This time, my services aren't needed.

Threads of green light bounce inside the wound. These magical sutures pull the wound back together on their own. I've never seen anything like it.

I was right. Dex has my green osmos power.

I check my pendant. The mirror world inside is still intact, showing the interior of my old Bartlebee home. Only now, Jocasta and Taryn are now joined by the rest of the Wulfhelm pack. Everyone's asleep, except for Taryn and Jocasta who stand watch over the sleeping shifters.

It's an idea at that. I should be asleep as well, only I'm too hyped up to rest. I keep stepping to the cave mouth, checking for any sign of Elise. Did I imagine she was outside before?

It's a large cave that's warm and dry. To kill time, I check the many trunks that Young Dex left behind. I'd already drained the water supplies for Wolf Dex. Other trunks contain leathers of all shapes and sizes. Many hold human books, magazines and music. There's even an old record player with a crank to play vinyl.

At the bottom of one trunk, I find a small box on which three words are written in tight script: *for my vita.*

My heart warms. I smile. Dex was thinking of me at the same time I was watching him. Both of us were missing the other, even though we'd never met.

As the hours pass, Wolf Dex curls into a circle. My adrenaline rush finally passes. I crawl into the center of Dex's cuddle loop. We're now cuddling in the same position, only one of us is a wolf. It's surprisingly comfy.

I fall asleep at last.

DEX

When I wake up, the breeze smells of sea salt and morning sunshine. Grayson lies curls up against me. I settle my chin onto my front paws. While I wait for Grayson to awaken, I think through everything that happened yesterday.

Grayson inhales and rolls over. "You're up."

"And thinking," I state.

"About?"

"My lands are overrun by the Prism Master. My pack is locked away. If there were ever a time to make wishes, it would be now." I tilt my head to meet Grayson's gaze. "Your six-old-your self was right. We should look for the three osmos mirrors."

Grayson sits up and wraps her arms around her legs.

"What about the Prism Master and Lady R? Won't they be tracking us?"

"They aren't yet. It's odd, but we can't worry about Lady R and the Prism Master. Perhaps they're scheming something for us. Or maybe they're afraid to go after the osmos mirrors."

"About those mirrors," I add. "People go after them all the time. They don't return. It's not a small thing to take on that quest. Maybe there's another way to fix things."

"I trust your prophecy, Grayson. It's too perfect for this situation not to be right."

Grayson's pendant always hangs on a chain around her her neck. She cups the small round mirror in her palms. The acidic scent of fear fills the air. "The pups..."

I sit up halfway. With my vision back, I can clearly see what's happening in the pendant. Some of the pups are coughing. Others lie on the ground, deep in sleep. Jocasta goes from pup to pup, trying to get them to take spoonfuls of some purple potion.

This isn't typical. My pups are up before dawn, running around in circles. If one or two are ill, their shifter healing fixes any problem within a few hours. Worry churns inside me.

"The poison mirror," whispers Grayson. "I didn't get them out in time."

"Can you heal them?"

"I'll try." Grayson grips the pendant. Closing her eyes, she scrunches up her face in concentration. A few green puffs of energy waft up from her hands, but they quickly dissipate.

"Anything?"

Grayson opens her eyes again. "No, I think my magic went to you." She takes the chain from her neck and offers me the pendant. "Do you want to try?"

At these words, fiery magic ignites inside me. Anger streams through me. *Someone threatens my pups.* I bare my teeth and growl. Lines of green smoke wind up from my nostrils.

The rage turns to a burning sense of fury. Animal rage courses through every muscle in my wolf's body. When I speak, my voice is a low and supernatural growl. "This magic is not for healing."

Grayson nods slowly. "I understand."

I force in deep breaths. "My power is for the Prism Master."

Grayson shivers. Power and magic emanate off her in waves. It's the wolf in her, answering the cry of my own animal. She steps over to meet my gaze straight on. When Grayson next speaks, her eyes shine with silver light.

"That's as it should be." Little by little, she rises to her full height. "Now, let's find those mirrors."

No question where to go next. The first osmos mirror is in Snow White's castle. Everyone knows where the place is, the secret is what happens to those who go inside. The Tulgey Wood, home to the original Alice in Wonderland, is only a few miles from the castle. that will be our second stop.

Rising onto all fours, I stretch out and shake my fur. "We can try Snow White's castle. It's the closest. The Tulgey Wood isn't much farther away."

"Snow White is the first mirror," says Grayson. "We should go there first or, you know…"

"No, I don't."

"I forget where I learned it." Grayson chuckles. "But mirrors can be very temperamental. It's like telling them your wish instead of asking for help. The first mirror might be jealous if we skip over it."

"In that case, Snow White's castle is a half-day's hike from here. We should go in human form. I've extra clothes in my boxes, if we need them." I follow this up with a smile.

"What has you so happy?"

"I'm a wolf. How can you tell I'm pleased?"

"Your grin is about three feet long."

"Ah, true. Both my beast and I consider this morning to be a good change of events."

Grayson sets her palm on her mirror pendant. "How so?"

"The magic of Wulfhelm is safe inside me." I stalk closer to Grayson. "And even better, you're starting to trust in your own power." Nuzzling her neck, I whisper in Grayson's ear.

"Now, let's head off on our adventure."

GRAYSON

*L*eaving his cave behind, Dex and I march along the beach. Both of us wear the basic brown leathers with straps—a standard uniform for Dex's branch of the Fortitude clan. We each tote a small pack with water and other supplies. As we march along, I check the skies for signs of Elise or her harpies.

Only the occasional seagull passes by.

I also scan the sky for any emerald mirrors being used for spying. Those will appear as a misty shape. An experienced snoop will hide their mirror on the outside of a cloud. I certainly did when I was checking on Dex. But Lady R and the Prism Master don't know much about mirrors. Their efforts would be pretty obvious.

Even so, there's no sign of any odd clouds. Which

means that we aren't being followed or watched. That should be a comfort.

Somehow, it isn't.

The beach gives way to more rocky ground. Dex and I start making our way up, down and around a range of magically dramatic cliffs.

Definitely Show White territory.

There's not a lot of chatter as we march along. This isn't like walking through Thornfield while discussing Glubby the goldfish. Both of us are lost in our thoughts. Dex is the one to break the silence.

"How well do you know the story of Snow White?"

"She's the classic fairy tale life template and..."

Dex shoots me a sideways glance. "And what?"

"I don't know if you have any Snow White besties. I mean, I know you, but I don't *know you*-know you, if that makes sense."

"It does make sense. You don't wish to offend. So you know, I have no Snow White besties."

I shrug. "In that case, Snow White is notorious for being sweet girl but a total dumbass."

"Humans believe Snow White recovered after eating the apple from the wicked witch." Dex smirks. He's pretty certain about what I'll say next, and I think he's looking forward to it.

"Okay, truth time. Humans think Snow White lived

happily ever after, but no one here buys it. Anyone who takes overly-perfect fruit from old crones simply won't last long in the Faerie Realm. I mean, I grew up in an isolated cabin and I know this stuff."

Dex chuckles. "Agreed." He has dimples when he smiles. Is it terrible that I want to skip Snow White's castle and just march around with Dex for a few days? Maybe, but I don't care.

"I don't get it," I add. "The mirror was used by Snow White's evil stepmother. Somehow, the chick who eats poisoned fruit ends up with both the mirror and castle. There's no sign of the prince, the huntsman, the evil queen, nothing. How did the sweetie pie dumbass end up with everything?"

"Maybe she's not as sweet as she seems."

The rocky ground leads upward. We crest a small hill to be greeted by a view that knocks the air from my lungs. There's a great valley before us and beyond that, Snow White's castle.

We're almost there.

Snow White's Castle

23

DEX

I'm glad to have my vision back for many reasons. One is certainly that I get to take in this view. Snow White's castle looks over the countryside in a way that's beautiful and predatory, all at once.

Grayson steps closer. "What's really happening in there?"

I wrap my arm around her shoulder, pulling Grayson against my side. Touching her helps to ground me, both man and wolf.

"The answer feels close," I state. "There's something bigger here that I'm not perceiving."

"Same here."

I take in a deep breath. "One way to find out."

A thin trail winds its way down the cliffside and into

the valley below. From there, it's a short hike up the mountain to Snow White's castle.

As we step along, there's no missing the signs of all the fae who made this trek before us. The path is well-worn. Messages are carved onto the nearby stones and trees. Grayson reads them off as we walk by.

"Bring me gold. Save my daughter. Kill my enemies." Grayson lets out a low whistle. "I've never seen anything like this."

"I used to see it all the time."

"When?"

"There was once an altar that marked the border between Wulfhelm and Refraction. Fae would often visit the Prism King and plead for the chance to wish on his mirrors."

"The quintessence gave him mirrors?"

"Not exactly. The Prism King would vet all the requests for wishes. The ones he approved went to the Osmos Queen. She'd make the right mirrors appear. People would make their wishes. The end."

Grayson snaps her fingers. "I think I heard about this. The mirrors would appear in a crystal chamber, right?"

I nod. "As for the altar, it looked like a great stone skull. Fae would leave little gifts or messages there, hoping for good luck with the Prism King. They wrote a lot of the same things we see here. Only there was one difference."

"What's that?"

"You'd see two trails, one for coming and another for going. Fae would pass each other in a great loop to the Prism King. There's only one path here."

"People go to Snow White's castle. They don't return." Grayson scrunches up her nose. "Everything smells so stale here. No one's tried this path in a while."

I kneel and take in a deep breath. "I do catch the scent of an ogress. It's a few months old now." I rise. "If she left, it was by a different path."

"The magic mirror can always open a portal for you to a different place. Maybe that's what's happening."

"We must be open to the best and plan for the worst," I state. "that's what Taryn always says."

Grayson checks the mirror pendant. "Taryn." She frowns.

"How's the pack?"

"Unchanged. At least, no one else is getting sick." Grayson pulls in the small round mirror for a closer look. "Jocasta's still giving them medicine, so I suppose that's good."

I've been so focused on the pack, I barely notice that we've finished the long trek up the mountainside. Now the great double doors to Snow White's castle loom before us.

Grayson knocks. "Hello?" Anyone there?"

No response.

I slam my fist against the heavy wood. "Hello?"

There's still no answer, but I do hear the faint tinkle of orchestral music. "I know that tune. It's the Hall of the Mountain King."

Grayson sniffs. "You talked about an ogress before. Does she smell like burned bacon?"

"She does." I lean in closer to the door and inhale. "You're right. Her scent is stronger here." I take in another breath. "And it's fresh. She's alive."

Rough screams echo through the closed door, followed by a woman's gravelly voice. "You said you'd make me beautiful."

"Did you hear that?" I ask.

"Yes. That must be the ogress."

Another voice reverberates through the closed door. This one is sweet and gentle. "And so you are… now."

Grayson shivers. "Mirror magic just passed through the air… Silver energy… Very powerful."

"Do you think the mirror just made the ogress beautiful?"

"It could be. This magic is too new for me to know."

A long moment of silence follows.

Creak!

The double doors swing open on their own. Grayson and I step into the castle. It's an ornate place with shining wood floors and stained glass windows. I can scent the ogress, but there's no sign of her. A long hallway ends in a massive ballroom. It's made from more oak and stained glass. A line of chandeliers dangles from the ceiling.

Half-way across the room, a slim woman lies on the floor, immobile in her silver gown. The scent of death hangs near her. No question about it.

That must be the ogress.

Near the body there stands another woman, only she's very much alive. She has pale skin, ruby lips and wears a formal dress. A silver crown is perched atop her head.

"Hello, I'm Snow White," she announces. "And if you want to wish on my mirror, you'll have to dance."

Suddenly, I know exactly what I forgot about this fairy tale. How could I have forgotten? I check the dead ogress. A weight of worry settles onto my shoulders.

The dead woman wears a pair of red dancing slippers.

Snow White

24

GRAYSON

Oh, crap.

In the original story of Snow White, the tale doesn't end with a poisoned apple. The evil queen returns with a pair of red ballet shoes. Show White puts them on and dances herself to death.

"We do want to make a wish on your mirror," I begin. "But I know my fairy tales. Red shoes are not a good idea, especially when a Snow White fairy tale life template is involved."

Snow White sets her fists on her hips. "My castle, my rules."

Dex gestures toward the very dead body. "It didn't work well for the ogress."

Snow White rolls her eyes. "She wanted to be beautiful. Look at her now. That ogress is gorgeous."

"And dead," adds Dex.

"If you want a wish, then you dance," says Snow White. "After a few songs, the mirror will appear and turn into a portal. You two walk inside and do your business. Once you're within, the mirror could open another portal for you to step out onto your perfect dream life... Or, it might spit you back into this ball-room to dance yourself to death."

Dex narrows his eyes. "Has anyone walked into the mirror and not come back to dance themselves to death?"

"Good question." Snow White taps her chin. "That would be no. But this is one of the original magic mirrors from the first osmos quintessence. It's not like it *can't* chuck you somewhere other than my ballroom."

I look to Dex. "These aren't great odds."

"Come on, now." Snow White moves to stand in a spot where she blocks our view of the dead body. "You two look powerful. Smart. Magical. I bet you're better than any other fae around. And you have a wish that you want more than anything, I can feel it. Make your wish. You'll be fine. Why, I bet the mirror will drop you off somewhere in the human realm as a king and queen."

"Why haven't *you* danced yourself to death?" Dex asks.

I shoot him a thumbs up. "Good question."

"A long time ago, I did agree to put on those horrible shoes. But then, I made a wish on the mirror."

I wince. "And you asked for something specific?"

"Of course. I asked that someone else wear the blasted shoes. And I stay alive, so long as people show up and want to take their chances on wishes."

"Yeah. about that." I hiss in a breath through my teeth. "Specific wishes are a bad idea. The mirror gets put out. It gives you what you want but with a terrible twist."

Snow White sighs. "The ogress lasted two months before she bought it. I was despairing that I'd finally have to dance."

"There's no one else here?" I ask.

"Oh, I already danced everyone else to death ages ago. My prince, my stepmother, you name it. I was starting to worry until you two showed up."

Dex frowns. "We haven't agreed to make a wish."

"That's the thing," says Snow White Sweetly. "Technically, you don't need to."

Boom!

The doors to the ballroom slam shut. Silver mist fills the air. *Magic.* The metallic haze congeals into the form of an orchestra, all of them wearing silver livery with matching instruments.

Show White gestures toward me. "Ladies first!"

The red shoes vanish from the ogress' feet and reappear on mine. For a few moments, the silk twitches as it takes the perfect shape to fit me. The orchestra strikes up a waltz.

I dance.

A few bars of music play. I waltz about in a circle. My movements are so smooth, it's like I've been ballroom dancing all my life. Mostly because my body is not my own. Some invisible force puppeteers me.

The music stops. I stand still once more.

"Well," I deadpan. "That was weird."

Pop, pop, pop!

More silver haze appears nearby. Every nerve ending in my body goes on alert. Little by little, the mist congeals into the form of a ten-foot-tall mirror. Where the reflection should be, there's an open passageway into darkness.

It's a reflex to try and pull the shoes off. They don't budge.

"Stop stalling," warns Snow White. "The portal won't stay open forever. You'll miss your chance to make a wish."

Dex takes my hand and leads me into the darkness. After we cross the threshold, our footsteps echo in odd ways. Light from the ballroom shines behind us, casting odd shadows onto the silver floor ahead.

Boom!

A door slams behind us, blocking out any light. A deep male voice echoes through the inky blackness.

"Mirror, mirror on the wall. Who's the fairest of them all?" says the man. "That's the question I always received in the past. What do you two wish from me today?"

"Only your help," I say simply. "In whatever way you see fit to give it."

"And you, wolf," adds the voice. "What do you wish?"

"The same," says Dex. "Please."

A pool of light appears before us. A figure steps into the brightness. I'd know that person anywhere.

"Who is that?" asks Dex.

My stomach sinks. "It's my sister, Opal."

"She doesn't look the same."

"This is before she became a Rapunzel. Back then, Opal attended the Sidhe Elf Academy. She always wore heavy makeup to hide what she called her blemishes and imperfections. Her hair is supposed to look like a crown."

Across the magical space, Opal rolls her eyes. "Well, get over here, Grayson. I can't wait forever."

I take a half-step backward, I don't want to talk to my sister.

Dex moves to stand at my side. "You're strong enough to do this," he says, his voice low and soothing.

I take his hand. "*We* are."

OPAL

25

GRAYSON

*H*and in hand with Dex, I approach Opal. Although I know I'm actually a seventeen-year-old, I feel like a little kid once more. For a long minute, Opal and I stare at each other. She doesn't seem to notice Dex at all.

Opal folds her arms over her chest and sniffs. "Well?"

"Um, hi."

"That's it?"

"Hi, Opal?"

My sister rolls her eyes. "You're so disrespectful. Every other osmos lives by the code, *the mirror reflects what an osmos protects*. You know what that means?"

"Osmos fae are supposed to honor the next quintessence."

Memories appear. Everyone thought my sister was

the next quintessence. The Sidhe Elf Academy was actually a palace in the clouds. Opal was bought there in a flying boat with an honor guard of elf royalty. Whenever she visited our home cave, children fought for the chance to throw rose petals under her feet.

No wonder she was so screwed up.

"You're…" Opal gulps at the air in a way that reminds me of a fish out of water. "I can't even find the word!"

"Precocious?" I offer.

Opal narrows her eyes. "What does that mean?"

"That I'm too smart for my age and I know it."

"You're too everything, Grayson. And you're an unimportant six-year-old girl who's not visiting the osmos ceremonial chamber today. I don't care if Queen Xao did send a note to Mom and Dad, insisting you join us."

I recall the vision I saw back in Dex's cabin. "But, I *do* go with you to visit Queen Xao."

"I wouldn't be so sure," counters Opal. "Besides, if you do join us, you'll have to wait in the reception room. It's a little green closet that's just the right size for a tiny wisp of a troll like you."

An image pops into my mind. It's myself as a girl, slipping past that green door with the mirror I cast. I look to Dex.

"The mirror's trying to show me something," I whisper. "Only, I don't know what it is."

"I get that feeling all the time." Dex gives my hand a gentle squeeze. "This is a version of Opal from before the ceremony went awry with Ishir and Xao. At this point, she must have been deep into scheming with the Prism Master. Maybe you can get some information."

"Right." I clear my throat. "Do you know the Prism Master?"

Not the most subtle question in the world, but it works.

"Who's a Prism Master?" asks Opal. "There's a prism king and a very nice osmos fae who's just been appointed to serve that royal as a Prism Apprentice."

"The Prism Apprentice, that's who I mean," I state. "Do you know him?"

"The Prism Apprentice is very kind and powerful, unlike you," says Opal. "He's been selected to join Alpha Ishir and Queen Xao in a very important ceremony, same as I have. You don't even know what it's about, that's how useless you are."

A chill runs across my skin. More memories appear. Lines of logic connect inside me. "I'm powerless."

"Yes, of course. Everyone knows you're nothing."

The many shards of memory congeal into a greater image. Understanding rolls over me. Maybe Opal is trying to make me feel powerless because she knows the opposite is true. I decide to test the theory.

"What if I don't believe you? Maybe I'm the powerful one. How will you ever stop me then?"

Opal reaches into the folds of her skirt and pulls out what looks like a single red rose. Only it's not a flower.

"You know what this is?" asks Opal.

"It's Queen Xao's magic wand," I state.

A satisfied grin winds Opal's mouth. "It's a rose wand, one of a handful in Faerie. And Queen Xao has been using hers to help me. The Queen pricks her finger with a thorn from this rose. After she waves the wand about, a little bit of her silver magic goes into me."

"That's like what happened at the Muster Tree," whispers Dex. "We created a loop between Wulfhelm, you and me."

"Queen Xao's only been giving me drops of power to help me along. But when the time is right, I'll get all the power."

"You drain Queen Xao?" I ask.

"No, silly. Why bother? Queen Xao doesn't have enough magic to make a decent mirror, let alone recharge Wulfhelm without an army of helpers." Opal steps closer. "No, I'm waiting until your silver osmos power comes in. When you're ripe and ready, I'll use this wand to drain you."

The words ricochet through my mind.

When you're ripe and ready, I'll use this wand to drain you.

The attack on Wulfhelm… how I lost my green osmos magic… the fact that silver power grows inside me… and this quest for mirrors and answers… what if it's all part of some greater plan for Opal/Lady R to drain me? That way, she can become the quintessence.

My body goes numb with shock. I'm barely aware of Opal and Dex, let alone the fact that the ground beneath me is not only silver, it's glowing with power.

It isn't until the floor turns liquid-soft that I realize what's happening. The mirror is done with us. We're being tossed out.

Dex and I tumble through darkness before landing back on the dance floor of Snow White's palace. The silver orchestra remains in place. The red shoes are still on my feet. Dex is in his human form, wearing a tuxedo. I'm in a bright red dress.

I guess if she's going to dance us to death, at least Snow White makes us do it in style.

"I knew you'd be back." Snow White smiles. "And how nice you both look in your new outfits."

The orchestra strikes up another waltz. Without willing my limbs to move, I begin to dance once more.

26

DEX

It's happening again. The orchestra strikes up. Grayson's face is the definition of misery as she dances.

My heart sinks. Grayson is my mate. I can't allow this to happen.

Our lost lives flicker before my eyes. There's the commitment ceremony we'll never have. The children we'll never meet. The home we'll never make together.

I've loved the familiar weight of Grayson on my back as we race through the forest. Even as a kid, I couldn't wait to meet my vita. Now that I've met Grayson, I can't let her go.

My wolf.

My mate.

Tears pool in her lovely green eyes. I stare at the red

shoes that won't stop moving until they take her life. As the delicate silk tightened around her feet, I'd never felt more helpless and enraged.

A chill of awareness crawls up my back. *What if there is a way to beat this curse?* I scan the delicate windows lining one wall of the ballroom. The only magical thing in this castle is the mirror. That stained glass is thin as paper. Even better, it overlooks the forest behind the castle.

A plan quickly forms. Hope lightens my soul as I rush onto the dance floor. Fortunately, a waltz is a rather easy dance, especially when you have natural coordination.

"Don't do this," says Grayson. "You need to save your strength for when it's your turn to dance."

Show White's been watching us the whole time. Now, she stalks closer. "What are you two whispering about?"

I spin Grayson so she blocks Snow White from reading my lips. "Remember when Ulliver's question about our commitment ceremony?"

Grayson frowns as we take another turn around the dance floor. After a full minute, her eyes widen.

"That's right, I remember." She looks down at her red slippers. "That could work."

Snow White races up to us. "Off the dance floor!" She grabs my upper arm. "Wait your turn!"

I easily shake off Snow White's grip. Pulling Grayson to me, I waltz in a circle so Grayson spins in the air. Focusing on my inner wolf, I will my fangs to descend. Twirling Grayson around once more, I bite down on her lip. The coppery tang of her blood fills my mouth.

Because Hiriah was right. We don't need a commitment ceremony to link our souls and wolves. The magic of mating bites comes from the blood, not the ritual or location. Two bites makes us mates and wolves.

One bite? That gets things started.

Without missing a dance step, Grayson's body extends. Fur erupts on her skin. Her face extends with a muzzle. Muscle bulks along her arms and torso. Her thigh muscles expand while her calves taper to small paws.

Grayson becomes the perfect balance of woman and wolf.

When the red shoes first appeared on Grayson's feet, they needed precious seconds to adjust to her size. Now that Grayson is part wolf, the ballet slippers fall away from Grayson's paws. All the while, the orchestra keeps playing.

For the first time in far too long, Grayson stands still.

I don't waste a moment. If there's any lag, the shoes might reattach to Grayson's new feet. Summoning my inner animal, I burst into my full form as a Brutus wolf. Grayson slides onto my back, same as always.

Crash!

I leap through the stained glass window and land on the forest floor beyond. As I speed away, there's no missing the cries of Snow White.

"It's not my turn! No! Someone else is coming soon!"

The orchestra strikes up. Snow White falls silent.

Chances are, there's no need to worry about further trouble from that particular Snow White. Still, the Tulgey Wood isn't far from this spot. I'm in no mood to take chances.

I race North until I reach a forest of twisted trees. A man steps out from behind a trunk to block our path. I dodge around him and speed forward.

"Don't go!" he cries. "I'm here to welcome you to the Tulgey Wood."

"Tulgey Wood," repeats Grayson. "If that's where we are, then the original Alice in Wonderland must be nearby. We should find out what he has to say."

Pausing, I step back through the oddly-shaped trees. A man stands near one of the larger arbors. He wears an outfit made of leaves and emerald leather. A pair of deer antlers project from his forehead.

I don't like him. At all.

It isn't the horns that set me off, though. After all, my friend Jacoby has a pair of his own. It's more the spontaneous offer of help. The Faerie Realm isn't known for altruism that doesn't end with an unpleasant death.

"Who are you?" I ask.

"Why, I'm Snow White's Huntsman." He bows slightly at the waist as he adds something rather unexpected.

"I'm here to lead you to the fabled mirror of Alice in Wonderland."

HUNTSMAN

27

GRAYSON

ow. This guy is the definition of sketchy.

I slide off Wolf Dex's back. Normally, I'd feel rather odd, considering how I'm half-shifted into wolf form and wearing a partly shredded red dress.

But this guy's wearing leaves and horns. We're on even footing here.

"What did you say your name is?" I ask.

Now, most folks wouldn't answer my question before asking some of their own.

What's with the red gown?

Where are your shoes?

Why are you half-shifted into a wolf?

I happen to know Taryn gets asked that last question all the time.

If this man is surprised I look rather wolfy, he doesn't show it.

"I'm the Huntsman," he repeats calmly. "I follow a Snow White fairy tale life template."

"You don't resemble the Huntsman from Snow White," states Wolf Dex.

"Really? I think I'm rather suited to the forest."

Wolf Dex and I share a quizzical look. Clearly, both of us have doubts about this guy.

"What's wrong with me?" asks the Huntsman.

"Well, where to start?" I snap my fingers. "I have it. There are big leaves on your thighs. That's not really how hunters dress. Shouldn't you wear leathers?"

The Huntsman lifts his chin. "You're being closed-minded. Leaves make the best camouflage."

"And you have horns sticking out of your head," adds Wolf Dex.

The Huntsman folds his arms over his chest. "Are you always this judgey?

"Okay," says Wolf Dex. "Let's agree for the sake of argument that you're a huntsman from Snow White. What are you doing leading people to the great osmos mirror of Wonderland?"

"Well, that's a story," says the Huntsman. "It's a long one. Do you have some time?"

"No," says Wolf Dex.

"In that case, I'll make it fast," states the Huntsman. "Everyone in the original Wonderland died years ago. This was unclaimed territory. I got tired of dealing with the original Snow White." He pulls an errant leaf off one of his horns. "Not sure if you heard, but she entered into a pact with her mirror."

"We heard," I state.

"The deal keeps her alive, but she's incredibly irritating to serve." The Huntsman takes on a whiny tone. "Come, meet my mistress. She'll dance you to death, but I can't tell you that."

"That wouldn't be any fun," I agree.

"I roamed around, looking for new employment. I soon found Wonderland deserted. Its mirror was abandoned. The way I see it, the Wonderland mirror wouldn't be so close to Snow White's castle if I weren't meant to protect it. Don't you think?"

"It's dangerous to assume why magic does anything." Wolf Dex looks to me and tilts his head. The question is there, although he doesn't say a word. *Should we follow him?*

I shrug. *Why not?*

"Do you accept guidance to Wonderland?" asks the Huntsman.

"Yes," I reply. "We do."

A slow and wicked smile curls across the Huntsman's

face. For the fraction of a second, the grin looks far too large for his human face, but the effect is gone too quickly to be certain.

"In that case, follow me." The Huntsman slips off deeper into the woods. He moves so quickly, it might be hard for most fae to follow him. Wolf Dex and I can follow him easily.

The Huntsman speeds through a maze of trees until reaching a dark pit in the earth. Turns out, this is the entrance to an underground tunnel. We follow the Huntsman through the subterranean passage until reaching a small clearing. This used to be a temple of some kind. Ruined bits of masonry litter the ground. One wall holds a round mosaic of a woman with a rabbit's head.

I gesture toward the image. "What's that?"

"Why the entrance to Wonderland, of course," replies the Huntsman. "When I speak the magic words, the picture-door opens."

Dex does a double take. "Wonderland is underground?"

"You fall for a time and then you reach it," says the Huntsman. "Don't you two read?"

"I know the story," I state. "This doesn't feel right, though."

"My apologies." The Huntsman sets his hand against

his heart in an overblown show of sadness. "It seems my reality doesn't match your precious feelings."

Dex and I share a long and frowny look. Neither of us trust the Huntsman—if that really is his identity—but we do need to make a wish from this mirror.

"Go on," says Dex. "Speak the words to open the door."

The Huntsman grins. Once again, there's the barest flash of an otherworldly and overlarge smile. He bows low as he speaks two final words.

"With pleasure."

Entrance to Wonderland

28

DEX

The Huntsman stands before the mosaic wall.

He raises his arms and proclaims in a loud voice: "Curiouser and curiouser."

The mosaic splits down the center in a jagged pattern. The two sides now open up. Since I'm still in my wolf form, it's natural to stalk closer to the opening. It's nothing more than a deep pit. Inhaling deeply, I catch the scent of old paper and a long-gone rabbit. There's also the smell of fresh grass and dead leaves. That's the Huntsman.

I swing my head around. "What's down here?" I ask.

"Wonderland, of course," says the Huntsman.

I'm glad that Grayson is still in her hybrid wolf form. She'll be in better shape in case of trouble.

"You two are such a jittery pair," says the Huntsman. "I'll go first." He races past us and leaps into the pit.

I turn to Grayson. "Still want to do this?"

"We have to find that mirror." Grayson grasps her pendant. "I just checked. They're getting worse."

Her words send a shiver of alarm across my shoulders. "Then climb on and get a good hold."

Grayson slips onto my back. There's a gentle tug against my skin as she takes a firm grasp of my fur. Her legs tighten against me.

With Grayson in place, I leap into the darkness.

We fall.

The darkness fades into a strange scene. Around us, the world fills with a shifting collection of books, clocks, and portraits of rabbits. Things tumble far more slowly than should be natural. Some of the objects warp and stretch as they fall. It's classic Alice in Wonderland.

So far, so good.

The objects around us turn larger. Some of the clocks became bigger than I am. Books are now held in neatly-packed shelves or large wooden chests. As we continue to fall, I twist about to avoid slamming into any of the big stuff.

The scent of fresh grass and dead leaves turns strong. "The Huntsman is close," says Grayson.

"I scent him as well," I state. "Only, the Huntsman jumped into the pit before us. How could he be close?"

"I see him," says Grayson. "He's far away, but closing in."

Sure enough, I spy the Huntsman. At first, he's a green dot that defies magical gravity to move toward us. As the Huntsman gets closer, I detect his trick—the man uses slow-falling objects as springboards to jump his way closer. He leaps from a wooden chest to an over-sized pocket watch to a tall set of bookshelves.

And all the while, the Huntsman is singing.

"Twas brillig, and the slithy toves
Did gyre and gimble in the wabe:
All mimsy were the borogoves,
And the mome raths outgrabe.

"Beware the Jabberwock, my son!
The jaws that bite, the claws that catch!
Beware the Jubjub bird, and shun
The frumious Bandersnatch!"

As a boy, I read all the Alice in Wonderland books written by the human, Lewis Carroll. I even had copies of them stowed in my cave retreat. This poem about the Jabberwock has always been a favorite passage of mine from that series. Yet, hearing the Huntsman sing it? A thread of unease winds through me.

The Huntsman jumps closer. "I knew you'd join me!"

"Where's the mirror?" I ask.

The Huntsman stops jumping when he's only a few yards away. Lacing his fingers behind his head, he lays back and allows himself to slowly descend at the same pace as me and Grayson.

"We'll find the mirror at the bottom of this fall," replies the Huntsman at length. "Only we must be careful. Alice made too many demands of her mirror. It turned on her and all of Wonderland. They're all dead down there. Have been for centuries. I chose a different path."

"And what path is that?" asks Grayson.

"Oh, I don't go anywhere near the thing. I merely use it as bait." The Huntsman grins, and there's something definitely inhuman about his smile. The Huntsman is changing. His pale skin turns leathery and gray. Fangs descend. Limbs lengthen. The set of deer antlers expands.

He's no longer the Huntsman.

I could be shocked, but my inner animal knew the truth all along.

This is the Jabberwock.

JABBERWOCK

29

GRAYSON

Talk about nasty.

The Huntsman was never my favorite-looking resident of Faerie. After this change, the guy would win an award for ugly.

"What do you want?" asks Wolf Dex.

The Jabberwock bares his many fangs. "If you want the mirror, you must get past me."

The Jabberwock doesn't wait for our reaction. He kicks off from a portrait of the white rabbit and leaps right toward me and Wolf Dex.

We launch into the oddest fight ever. Wolf Dex and I jump away at the last moment. The Jabberwock swipes at us, but his attack is too slow to connect.

Wolf Dex and I land on a large bookcase. An oversized pocket watch floats by.

That could be useful.

Grabbing the timepiece, I chuck it at the Jabberwock's head. Since I'm still partly-shifted, my aim is rather good. I clock the Jabberwock on the side of his skull. He's injured, but not unconscious.

The Jabberwock keeps attacking. We evade. The battle goes on and on. Wolf Dex tries to counter-attack, but the Jabberwock is too experienced at this game. The moment we leap in his direction, the Jabberwock has already lurched out of our path. It strikes me that we could get stuck this way, with the Jabberwock forever trying to kill us.

It's a rather *Alice in Wonderland way* to spend eternity.

At last, a marble bust of the Mad Hatter floats by.

That'll do it.

I pluck the stone carving out of the air and throw it at the Jabberwock with all my might. It lands another blow, this time at the back of the Jabberwock's head. His body goes limp.

"Unconscious or dead?" I ask.

"Hard to tell," says Wolf Dex.

Everything around us pauses, from the bookshelves and paintings to the pocket watches and bunny fluff. Since we walked through the mosaic doors, this pit has been subject to an odd kind of gravity.

With the end of our battle with the Jabberwock, regular rules of nature come back into play.

Everything tumbles.

"Hold on!" cries Wolf Dex.

We fall for what seems like ever. As we go lower, a bookshelf flashes with light before disappearing. Then a painting goes bright before getting eradicated. My now-favorite bust of the Mad Hatter flares and disappears. .

Everything's disappearing. *Will we be next?*

It feels like we're hurtling toward the ground. At the last moment, our fall slows. Wolf Dex and I gently touch down.

It takes a few moments for my eyes to adjust to the dim light. We've landed in a forest clearing. A long table stands nearby. Its surface is covered in teacups, pots and dust. Skeletons sit on the chairs. One wears a blue dress. Another has an overly-large top hat. Although everything is covered in cobwebs, there's no missing who these bones once belonged to: Alice and the Mad Hatter.

The Jabberwock may have lied about his initial appearance, but in this, at least, he told the truth. Here's the original Alice, long dead. Dex steps closer. "Did you see this?"

I move to stand at his side. Clasped in Alice's right hand is a red rose wand. My eyes widen. "That's exactly like Xao's mirror wand."

"Why would Alice have one?" asks Wolf Dex,

"Perhaps she wanted to do the same thing as Opal—to drain its power." I tilt my head and consider. "The question is, did her attempt to drain the magic from the mirror work?"

Wolf Dex grins. "If Alice did take all the magic, it didn't do her any good."

"Which means the mirror must have won." I turn around in a slow circle, scanning the nearby forest.

Nothing but trees.

I frown. "If the mirror won, then where is it?"

Pop, pop, pop!

A wall of silver mist materializes nearby. My breath catches. A great frame takes shape nearby. It's a square number made of silver and carved with images of the white rabbit's head. The interior of the mirror is dark and open.

Another tunnel, just like what happened in Snow White's ballroom.

I stay in my partly-shifted form. Dex remains a great wolf. There's no need for us to discuss what to do next. Together, we step over the mirror's frame and into the darkness. Once we're deep inside, all light vanishes. An old woman's voice echoes through the inky black.

"Alice asked me for all the magic of Wonderland," says the mirror. "What do you want?"

I grasp the pendant. "Help."

"Whatever you can give," adds Wolf Dex.

Like the mirror in Snow White's castle, a light appears far ahead. Wolf Dex and I follow it until we step out onto another clearing in the woods. The air here carries a familiar scent.

We're on pack land, or near it.

A great stone altar looms before us. The center of the structure is carved into the shape of a human skull.

"I know this place," says Wolf Dex. "This is Fortune's Altar, the place where pilgrims would stop on their way to the Prism King's palace. They'd make offerings and hope for good luck with getting a wish from a magic mirror. This is Refraction territory. We're near the border to Wulfhelm."

"What happened to the altar?" I ask. "I've never seen it before."

"*He* happened," says Wolf Dex.

I'm about to ask who he is when a figure steps up to the altar. The man wears white robes and carries a small lamp. I know those long blond tresses anywhere.

"It's the Prism Master," I whisper.

"Not yet," says Dex. "We've gone back in time. This moment takes place before the ceremony that killed Xao and Ishir. He hasn't stolen all those mirrors and taken over the palace."

"So, you met him?"

"Once. It was right after I arrived in Wulfhelm." When Wolf Dex next speaks, his voice carries a low growl.

"This is the Prism Apprentice."

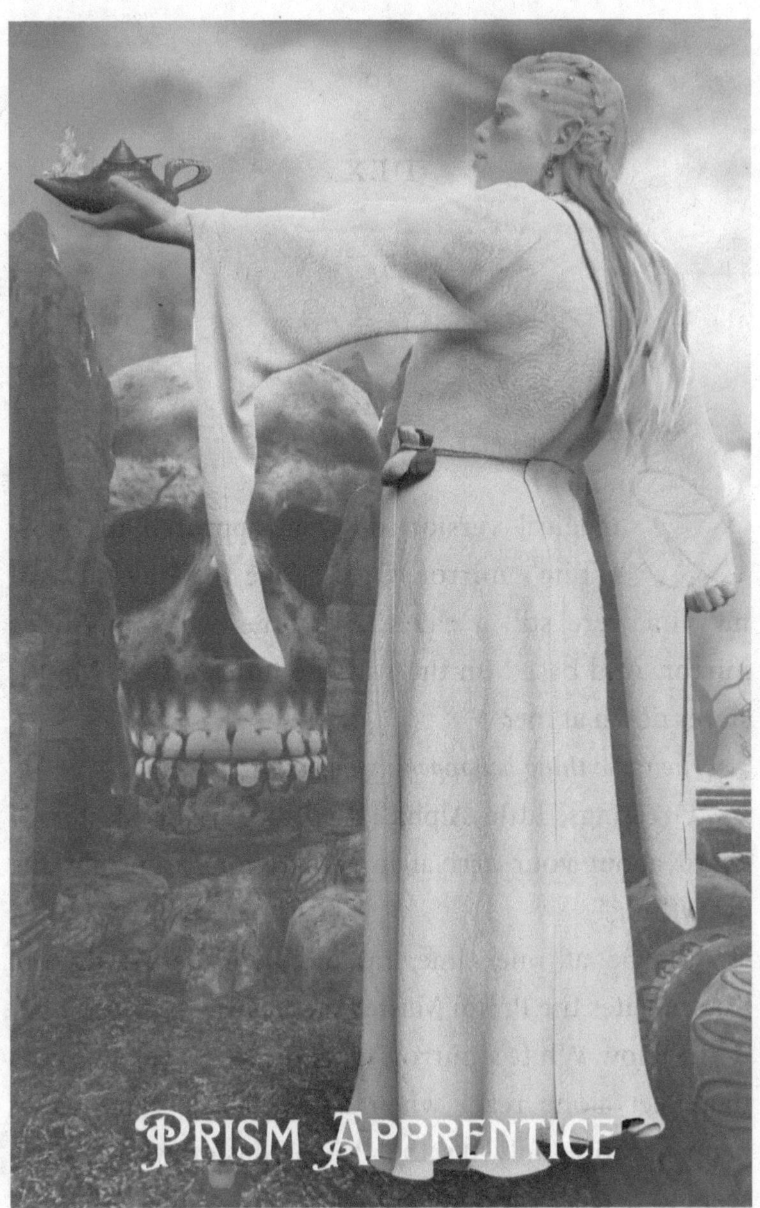

PRISM APPRENTICE

DEX

A magical version of Opal appeared in Snow White's mirror. Opal spoke to Grayson as if my vita were still a child. This time, we're in Alice's mirror. And based on the way the future Prism Master stares down at me?

The same thing is happening again.

"Greetings, little Alpha," says the Prism Master. "I heard about your arrival in Wulfhelm. Taryn tells me everything."

"Maybe at one time, he did," whispers Grayson. "Taryn hates the Prism Master these days."

In Snow White's mirror, Opal didn't recognize I was there, let alone react when I spoke. The same thing happens now, only it's the Prism Master who doesn't seem to detect Grayson.

Over years of dealing with this fellow, I've learned that the Prism Master will reveal almost every secret in his noggin, if he's given enough room to do so. Best to lead with open-ended questions.

"You have me at a disadvantage," I state, knowing how he loves being told of his superiority. "Who are you?"

"I'm an osmos fae. Surely, you've heard of me."

"Not yet," I state.

"I used to keep records of all Queen Xao's mirrors." The future Prism Master speaks those words through a sneer. Clearly, he sees record-keeping as beneath him. "Now, the Prism King has me as his assistant. Since I know all the mirrors, I can help vet *which* magical reflection goes best with *what* wish." He raises the lamp. "And you must know about the spell in this fire."

I hate playing to the Prism Master's sense of superiority, but I do love the results when he spills information.

"Again, you have me at a disadvantage."

"This lamp wields the crimson fire of the osmos. It's perfect for the task the ailing Prism King gave me today." The Prism Master gestures toward the altar. "The king sees ritual sacrifice as demeaning to those who come to beg for wishes from Queen Xao's mirrors. Imagine! Fae leave coins and messages here, when they should be giving their gifts and praise to the king directly."

"I've heard about the Prism King," I state. "I don't think he wants gifts and praise. He sees his osmos duty as making sure the best wishes are granted."

"He's a fool," snarls the future Prism Master. "As is his daughter, Captain Zoya. She will never be queen."

I can flatter when necessary, but there are limits. One of them is bad-mouthing Zoya. She's been loyal to her people. In this case, that means serving the Prism Master even while she loathes him.

"Strong words," I declare. "Speak that way and the king will punish you. What will you do then?"

The Prism Master smirks. "Nothing. I'll be the king's role before long. You'll see! When the crystal chamber returns, fae from across Faerie will plead for the chance to make wishes. I'll give magic and get paid for it. I've a question for you, though. Will you stop me?"

I do a double-take. "I'm a kid. How do you expect me to do that?"

I know the Prism Master. He's a blabbermouth, but he isn't wrong. If the man suspects I can end his plans, then there's a way it can happen.

The Prism Master's smirk expands into a smug grin. "Have you heard who will be at the ceremony? The newest Rapunzel shall attend. She appeared after Alpha Ishir and Queen Xao died. You might like her."

There's a trick in his logic, but I can't quite see it. The Prism Master is fishing around to see if I know something. *Again.*

I run a quick timeline of where this magic mirror has taken me and Grayson. This version of the Prism Master has just killed Ishir and Queen Xao… and helped Grayson's sister, Opal, to become a Rapunzel. At the same time, my younger self has just arrived at Wulfhelm and met Taryn. Again, I sense a larger pattern, but don't see it clearly.

"There's something more here," I tell Grayson.

"I always knew that Lady R wanted to have you as her prince," offers Grayson. "Maybe the mirror is trying to show you that he was pushing you two together in the past?"

"Perhaps," I state. "I can't shake the sense it's something else."

Prism Master all out-laughs. "It's clear you know nothing. How perfect." He tosses the lamp at the altar. Red mist instantly surrounds the structure. Low hissing noises fill the air. Fast as a whip, flames erupt around the altar. The shade of fire is so crimson and bright, it's clearly magic.

Within seconds, the altar is burnt down to nothing.

Most altars are built upon sacred burial sites. When the osmos fire dies down, all that remains on the spot are a set of old bones.

Just like Alice and the Mad Hatter.

That important realization feels closer than ever. Even so, it remains out of reach.

GRAYSON

The view of the Prism Master collapses into a square image that's framed by darkness. The picture zooms away from us until it's only a pinprick of light in a sea of darkness.

Then, it's gone.

Wolf Dex and I no longer visit the past. Now, we wait in perfect darkness. When this has happened before, a disembodied voice spoke to us. That doesn't happen this time. Still, the hair on the back of my neck stands on end.

Someone watches. Listens. It's definitely the mirror.

"Hello?" I ask. "Are you there?"

"I didn't hear any popping," says Wolf Dex. "That means our wish isn't over. The mirror is still here."

A deep male voice echoes through the air. "I helped you. So did Snow White's mirror. It's time to thank us."

"Uh, thanks?" I ask.

No reply.

Darkness still surrounds us.

This is what I mean about magic mirrors. They're total prima donnas. Maybe I need to suck up a little more.

I clear my throat. "I want to thank Snow White's mirror for doing such a great job."

"At?" urges the mirror voice.

"Well." I exhale slowly and think fast. "Snow White's mirror gave me a chance to talk to Lady R back when she was just my evil sister. It helps to see how Opal got her hands on a rose wand. I didn't realize there were so many of those out there."

"And?" urges the voice once more.

"And I saw another rose wand with Alice," I add. "So that's pretty great."

"I didn't just help you," adds the voice. "What about your wolf?"

"It was useful to see the Prism Master before he got power," says Wolf Dex. "Wow, was that ever helpful."

"I scent your mistruth," says the mirror. "Do not hold back your full opinion from me. That's disrespectful."

"I do know you helped me in that visit with the Prism Master," adds Wolf Dex. "I just haven't figured out some things yet. It's nothing on you and your amazing magical powers."

Long seconds pass before the mirror speaks again. "Your gratitude is acceptable. Just remember how much these first two mirrors have done for you. The next mirror is pampered. The rest of us don't think it's fair."

"Absolutely." I force on a smile. "You two are great. Thanks ever so much."

Pop, pop, pop!

A square of light opens nearby. After being in such perfect darkness, it takes time for my eyes to adjust. The mirror is ending our wish. Unlike the Snow White mirror, we aren't being deposited back in Wonderland.

Instead, we're being led somewhere else entirely.

Wolf Dex and I step through the exit. Before us, there looms a series of concentric castle walls. In the center of these round structures, there stands a stone tower with a single window.

Wolf Dex inhales deeply. "It's night here. We're on the other side of Faerie.".

There's no need for him to say anything else. We both know where the mirror dropped us off.

We're at the tower of the original Rapunzel.

RAPUNZEL'S TOWER

DEX

he original Rapunzel's tower. We're really here. I can't believe it.

And our location isn't the only surprise. Back when Grayson and I stepped out of Snow White's mirror, both of us were magically changed into formalwear. This time, we've been returned to our human form and wearing black Wulfhelm leathers.

It's a crazy situation, but I still take the moment to celebrate seeing Grayson in the classic Wulfhelm look: leather pants, fitted jacket, hefty boots, and short cape.

She looks perfect.

Grayson looks me over from head to toe. "You look good yourself, Dex."

I wink. "Thank you."

"Guess we said the right thing to the last mirror."

"If confessing I have no idea what I'm doing is the right thing, then I certainly did it." I gesture toward her pendant. "How fares the pack?"

Grayson looks down into the mirror. I scent sorrow rolling off her. "The pups are unconscious. Some are panting. Others are breathing shallowly. A few froth at the mouth. Jocasta and Taryn are worried out of their minds. I don't know..." She doesn't finish the thought.

She doesn't need to.

I step closer and look into the pendant. Sorrow, rage and fear battle it out inside me. A dozen questions zing through my mind at once.

How could I let this happen?

Why would the Prism Master do this to innocent pups?

What can I do save them?

The last question jars me into action. "The best thing we can do now is find that last mirror."

Grayson nods. "It should be stored in the most secure place possible."

"That means it's hanging in the top room of the tower. We must breach the outer wall." I chuckle. "That may mean destroying our new outfits, though."

"Hey, I carry my own fur coat now." Grayson shoots me a sideways glance. "Whatever happens is fine, so long as we heal the pups."

A warm sense of pride seeps across my ribcage.

Grayson is acting more like a vita by the day. "The field is wider on the north side of the walls. That's where an entrance would be."

Grayson and I head off in that direction. At first, we move slowly. All our senses stay on high alert. After what happened with the last two mirrors, there's no point marching into danger.

We soon reach the main gate. It's open.

So. Strange.

With careful steps, we pass through the gate and into a wide and empty space. The next concentric wall stands nearby. Between the two battlements, the ground is well-trodden by heavy boots. Warriors have been here recently. A low silver mist hangs in the air.

I inhale deeply. There's no scent. Not that there were any strong smells outside the walls. However, that didn't seem so odd before, since there was a breeze outside the gate.

Now, we're within the high battlements. There should definitely be some smells from whoever runs this place.

There's nothing.

I reach out into an especially heavy patch of mist. The moment my skin touches the haze, the green power within me springs to life. I turn to Grayson. "Are you getting this?"

My vita stands nearby. Her fingertips brush the same patch of silvery haze. "This is osmos magic. It's blocking the scents in here. It might be doing something else, too. It's hard to tell."

"One thing is for certain," I state. "They knew we were coming. Hiding their scent means concealing their true identity."

"Do you think it's dangerous?"

"Not yet. If whoever runs this tower wanted to attack us, then we'd be dead already."

Grayson points across the clearing. "There's the gateway through the second wall," says Grayson. "It's open as well."

I tally what happening. "Pack leathers. Open gates. The warriors are gone."

"This is as strange as what happened with the Huntsman, but it doesn't feel as risky."

"True," I confirm. "But we should still be cautious. I think we can move more quickly, though."

Grayson and I step through the second wall. There's another open space between that inner barrier and the tower itself.

Like everything else here, the door to the tower is wide open. There's no sign of any warriors. The mist gets heavier.

We enter the tower itself. It's a hollow structure with

a thin staircase that winds inside the building. We hike up the steps until reaching a heavy wooden platform.

"This is it," I announce. "The tallest room in the tower."

A square wooden door has been cut into the panel of wood above my head. I touch the handle gently. The door springs back on its own. I shimmy through first, followed by Grayson.

We slip through into a tall room that's decorated with gray stone filigree. A single glass window looks out from one wall. A storm rolls in. Thunder rumbles through the air. A flash of lightning reveals a woman standing beside the stained glass.

The harpy, Elise.

ELISE

GRAYSON

I can't believe what I'm seeing.

This is the tower of the original Rapunzel. Elise stands before me. She wears a long red dress and a look that says she's assessing the situation. It all seems real, but you never know when it comes to the Faerie Realm.

I take a half-step closer. "Elise?"

"Greetings, Grayson." Elise opens her arms.

I can't help it. After so much disappointment and drama, I'm thrilled to have something good happen. I rush in for a hug. Elise gives the best embraces—her hugs involve both arms and wings.

"You said we'd see you again soon," I recall. "I'm so glad you're here."

Dex nods in Elise's direction. "You've protected Grayson. Thank you."

Elise breaks the hug and steps back. "You're most welcome."

"What magic brought you here?" I ask.

"The original Rapunzel was a harpy. She passed away centuries ago. Her mirror has stayed property of the crown."

I do a double-take. "You're Queen of the Harpies?"

Elise winks. "Didn't I mention that?"

"No," declares Dex.

"My title and mirror are secrets. Otherwise, I'd be swamped with fae looking to make wishes and get favors. If you'd been anyone else, you wouldn't have gotten anywhere near the first gate."

"If you're queen, then where are your warriors?" asks Dex.

"We'll get to that in a bit," replies Elise.

I step around in a circle. "There's no sign of a mirror."

Elise's face takes on a serious look—it's the one she uses when I must accept that I can't save a lupine pup. "The mirror remains hidden for now."

My pulse speeds. "What's wrong?"

Dex moves to stand beside me. "This will be like the

other mirrors. Elise will allow us a wish, but we must do something first."

"Correct," says Elise. "I've always cherished pups. It's how I met you, Grayson. One day, I looked in my mirror and asked it where I could find a lupine in need. And it showed me. I saw a little village of fae run by..." She naps her fingers, trying to remember.

"Mayor Primrose," I finish.

Elise smiles. "That's right."

"I remember that night," I continue. "I'd snuck away from my root heart to a border village between Faerie and the human world. Lupines are drawn there, so I'd check the place regularly. And this night, Mayor Primrose was hiding an injured lupine, but refused to let me heal the pup. Then, you appeared."

"It was the original time we teamed up," added Elise. "The first of many."

Dex sets his hand on my shoulders. "I appreciate everything you've done with Grayson. But, we have time limits here." Dex gestures toward my pendant.

"I know about your pups in that mirror, as well as how Taryn and Jocasta are within and trying to care for them." Elise steeples her hands under her chin. "You must have wondered why the Prism Master hasn't been chasing you from mirror to mirror."

"It occurred to us," says Dex.

"After I helped you escape, I approached Lady R and the Prism Master."

I nod slowly. "When you flew back toward the Prism Master, you made sure we saw you."

"And you came to the cave as well," adds Dex.

"To check that you'd survived," says Elise. "After I was sure you were on your way, I brokered a deal with the Prism Master and Lady R. If you agree to my bargain, it will be your wish."

My skin prickles over with gooseflesh. "What kind of deal?"

"If you two willingly return to Refraction, then I can save the pups and place them somewhere safe."

"Where?" asks Dex.

"You may have noticed that Prince Jacoby and I were working together during your escape. My mirror will heal the pups and move them to Jacoby's estate. They'll be safe there."

Dex shakes his head. "For how long? You can't trust the Prism Master. You have one magic mirror. He has dozens."

"My warriors are at Jacoby's estate now, ready to receive your pack. I'm placing my own people at risk, same as yours. I'm banking that the Prism Master and Lady R will be too distracted by the both of you to focus on the pups right away. My people will fly the pups to a third location as soon as possible."

I check my mirror-pendant again. All the pups are immobile. Maybe it's my newly-awakened wolf senses, but I know one thing for certain. *Our pack is dying.* I picture Ulliver strutting about in his formal leathers... Hiriah cuddling Snowball... and all the other pups running and yipping through the halls of Thornfield. My eyes sting with held-in tears.

I hand over the mirror pendant to Dex. He scans it as well. There's no need for us to have a discussion. We both know what to do.

"You can heal them all and keep them safe?" asks Dex.

"My bargain only extends to the teachers and pups. Taryn and Jocasta must stay in the mirror. Lady R insisted, saying that Jocasta ran away for too long. She's not setting her free now."

Dex and I share a long look. Dex is the one to break the silence. "Jocasta and Taryn wouldn't want to be freed if it meant the pups died."

Elise nods. "You've made the right decision. As queen, I've been able to watch you both for a long while."

A haze of silver smoke materializes nearby. The mist solidifies into a twelve-foot-tall mirror. Images appear inside the reflection. There's Professor Tallon's house… my old root heart home… the Estuary where Dex was born… and Wulfhelm.

"We met the other mirrors," I report. I think back to the questioning that Dex and I received from Alice's mirror. "How do I say this? They seemed jealous of yours. Why?"

"They didn't *seem* jealous, they are," says Elise. "Snow White served her mirror. Alice tried to destroy hers. My mirror and I are partners. It's not always easy. Take this situation, for instance. I didn't only make a bargain with the Prism Master and Lady R. My mirror wanted to know if you'd put the pups' fate before your own. Only then would it consider helping you."

"This was all a test," says Dex.

"Yes," confirms Elise. "And so far, you've passed. Now, you know everything. Do you still wish the mirror's help?"

Dex and I share our longest look yet before speaking a single word in unison.

"Yes."

DEX

$\mathcal{E}$lise exhales. "You've done the right thing."

Grayson slowly pulls the pendant's chain over her head. Holding the small round mirror in her hands, my vita crosses the room. Every step she takes closer to Elise, my pulse speeds faster.

I hate the idea of placing my pack in the hands of anyone, even if that person is Queen of the Harpies.

With hesitant movements, Grayson sets the pendant onto Elise's outstretched palm.

"Thank you," says Elise. She steps over to the mirror and sets the pendant against the reflective surface.

The mirror changes. Instead of showing a white haze, the reflective surface now shows the exterior behind Jacoby's cottage. It's a lavish garden with multicolored flowers of every kind. One by one, the pups materialize on the grass.

I suck in a shaky breath. *Please, let the pups get better.*

For her part, Grayson leans her back against my chest. I sense her pulse speed as well.

As each pup appears, their bodies flare with silver light. The little ones twitch a few times. An electric jolt of worry moves through me.

Will they get well?

Seconds pass before something amazing happens. The silver light and magic vanish from the pups. Once the silver power is gone, the pups leap to their feet and trot about.

A weight of worry seeps from my shoulders. *This is working. The mirror is healing my pack.*

As each pup recovers, a harpy kneels before the little one. The pair chat for a bit. As a rule, my pack is an untrusting bunch. But these pups leap into the harpies' arms. The women unfurl their wings and take the pups into the air.

"That's amazing," I whisper. "I've never seen them trust anyone so quickly."

"Harpies are great with pups," says Grayson.

Last to appear in the cottage garden are the teachers. When the pendant holds only Taryn and Jocasta, Elise returns the little mirror to Grayson.

"Don't worry," says Elise. "Taryn and Jocasta are safe and healthy. If anything, they can rest now that they aren't caring for the sick."

"Even Taryn?" asks Dex. "He was still recovering from burns."

"Yes, even him," confirms Elise. "The mirror took care of any lingering injuries."

Grayson resets the pendant chain around her neck. "Thank you."

Elise slowly scans me and Grayson. "I wouldn't do this if I didn't know you two can come out of this. Do you believe that?"

My breath catches. *Does Grayson know her power yet?*

"We can try," says Grayson.

Not yet, but she will.

"In that case, it's time for *me* to make *your* wish." Elise turns to the mirror. "They need your help. What will you do?"

The mirror's interior changes again. This time, it shows the landscape of the Prism Master's realm. *Refraction.* Sometimes, the Prism Master is able to hide the real state of his territory. This mirror shows things as they truly are.

A wasteland.

Things weren't always a rocky desert. Back when I

was a pup, the ground still held scrub brush and a few dying trees. Now, Refraction is a total ruin.

"What will the Prism Master do when we return?" asks Grayson.

"The Prism Master loves viewing parties," I explain. "This is where he shows off his castle and power. This time, the Prism Master will create what's called a crystal chamber."

"Right." Grayson nods slowly. "The Prism Apprentice mentioned that when we saw him in the mirror."

"Usually, the crystal chamber is used to show off mirrors to those pleading for wishes," I explain. "This time, the chamber will show off his latest sign of the Prism Master's power—having us as prisoners. He'll see if he can make any deals or gold from our demise."

All this while, I've had my arms wrapped around Grayson's waist. Now, she sets her hands on top of mine and grips them tightly. I sent the salty tang of sweat.

Grayson is afraid.

"Don't worry," I state. "I still believe you're a match for anyone."

Grayson takes in a deep breath. "I hope so."

Hand in hand, we step through the mirror and into Refraction.

Refraction

35

DEX

"I still believe you're a match for anyone."

"I hope so."

Our last words still echo through my mind as Grayson and I step through the Rapunzel mirror and onto the ruined ground of Refraction.

Grayson wants to *believe* she has strength. I *know* she does. If I trust in anything in this life, it will be this.

As we step across the dry earth, a rough wind whips past us. I can't help but picture how these lands used to look. It wasn't perfect, but it wasn't a desert, either.

"There's no sign of the Prism Master or Lady R," I declare. "I'm in no mood to wait for them."

Grayson gives my hand a squeeze. "They're probably at Wulfhelm right now, picking out curtains."

I scan the horizon. "If we go West, we'll reach neutral territory. Do you feel ready to run?"

Before Grayson can answer, the ground shimmies. Long cracks form in the dried earth.

Crash!

Another mirror breaks through the ground. This one is as large as the others. The reflective surface is filled with white haze while its frame is made from pale crystals.

Grayson gasps. "I've never seen a mirror like that before."

"I have. It forms the crystal chamber."

We start to run West, but another crystal breaks through the ground. This one is large as the old Muster Tree.

Grayson and I switch directions and run East. Even more great crystals erupt from the earth. No matter which way we turn, we're blocked. My heart thuds with such fury, I hear the whoosh of my pulse.

In a final effort, we try to double back to where the Rapunzel mirror once stood. It's gone. And even if it were still around, Grayson and I aren't moving anymore.

Hefty white crystals have popped up from the

ground, one each for me and Grayson. At first, the great stones have the consistency of cement as they ooze around our legs. Then they turn solid, locking us in place from the knees down. I writhe against the new bindings, but it's no use.

More crystals erupt from the dry earth, creating a box-like structure around us. Crystals drip down from the ceiling. Others jut up from the ground. In the center of the room, there stands the great crystal mirror. Its main surface still shows a swirl of white haze.

A chill of recognition moves through me. "The crystal chamber is being built around us."

Grayson pales. "You mean, the same one where the old Prism King would listen to fae supplicants who wanted a wish?"

"The same," I reply. "Only, I don't think the Prism Master will use it that way."

The crystal mirror flares with white light. An image takes shape in the center.

It's the Prism Master.

He wears his black silk robes and an evil smile on his smug face. "Greetings." He steps through the mirror and into the great crystal chamber itself. Once he's in front of me, the Prism Master pauses.

"This is between us," I state. "Let Grayson go."

"How I've longed to say this to you," says the Prism

Master with a sigh. "It's all over. You're a fool. So is Elise. I'm about to break all my promises. And no one can say or do a thing about it. You know why?" In classic Prism Master fashion, he goes on to answer his own question. "Because I've got all the mirrors and power."

Hundreds of crystals now decorate the ceiling and floor in a jagged pattern. Before, two crystals had appeared and trapped me and Grayson from the knees down. Now that happens again in a different way and on a mass scale.

One by one, the crystals light up. As they do so, a different figure appears inside each clear stone. There's Ulliver. Hiriah. Taryn. Jocasta. Unlike the rocks that are trapping me and Grayson, the other crystals are empty.

And they're being used as prisons.

"What are you doing?" cries Grayson.

"I'm jailing up others just as I did you," says the Prism Master smoothly. "What did you expect?"

The terrified pups slam their bodies against the walls of their tiny prisons. Nothing works.

More crystals light up. Harpies appear inside these small dungeons. Then minotaurs. Jacoby. Zoya. Somehow, the Prism Master even dragged in Elise and her harpies.

Soon, every crystal is filled with a prisoner. My body turns numb with shock.

The Prism Master gestures across the scene. "Know this. The prisoners will watch you die before I kill them all as well. It's a fitting end, after all you've done to me."

"And what is that?" I ask.

When the Prism Master next speaks, his voice drips with menace. "You exist."

Once more, I have the familiar sense of a larger pattern that I simply cannot see. And that failure will not only cost me my life.

I'll lose everyone I love as well.

36

GRAYSON

"I still believe you're a match for anyone."

Before, I never felt those words were right before. That's even less true now. My skin chills over as I scan all the crystals around me. The Prism Master planned this out so well. He wants to hurt not only me and Dex, but everyone we care about. Despair presses in around me, heavy as a vise.

The main crystal mirror lights up again. An image appears on the central mirror. This time, it's Lady R. She wears a long red dress and an expression of sheer contempt. She strides over to stop before me.

"From the time you were born, it was clear you'd be the next quintessence and Osmos Queen," begins Lady R. "Do you know what that meant? Because I was destined to be the future quintessence and queen, people tossed rose petals onto my path... even in the Sidhe Academy. And those are high elves!"

"If you wanted my powers that badly, you could have asked."

"Bah," Lady R sneers. "You say you don't want power, but that's only another lie you tell yourself. When the moment comes, you'd never give up osmos magic. And I'm here today to tell you the truth. That power was never yours to begin with. That's why I had to convince you not to get attached to it.'"

"Attached? You knew I was the next quintessence and tried to brainwash me that I wasn't?"

"Because the power inside you is really *mine*. Everything that happened to you is for a reason. You're my little wooly lamb whose coat must be sheared."

"What do you want?" demands Dex. "If it frees Grayson and my pack, I'll do it."

Lady R saunters over to Dex. "Too bad, so sad. We could have been a couple. Now, I don't think you'll live out the day." She focuses on the Prism Master. "Isn't that right, darling?"

"No, his survival is rather unlikely."

"Back to you." Lady R saunters over to me while pulling something out from the folds of her robes.

A rose wand.

The crystal trap rises higher around me, locking me in up to my torso. Moving with supernatural speed, Lady R presses one of the rose wand's thorns against my hand. Blood pools on my palm.

She waves the wand over my wound.

Suddenly, silver ribbons of power flow out of my hand and go into Lady R's palm. Power drains from me and moves into my sister. I grit my teeth, trying not to scream. It isn't easy. Pain burns up my arm and radiates through my body.

Seconds pass, each one feeling as long as a year. My legs turn rubbery beneath me. White spots cloud my vision. I'm vaguely aware of all the pups weeping in their crystal cages. Dex stares at me, his face the definition of misery.

I don't have much longer.

DEX

Anger and despair overwhelm my mind. "How can you do this?" I call to the Prism Master.

"I told you," he replies smoothly. "You're very existence is an insult to me."

At last, the pieces of the puzzle fall into place. With a flash of insight, I know why the Prism Master hates me so much… the reason why Taryn was never part of the ritual to rejuvenate Wulfhelm… and what happened to Wyatt, the Alpha who has supposed to take over Wulfhelm after Ishir died.

"You," I say slowly. "I know your name."

The Prism Master waves his hand airily. "Of course, you do."

"I didn't before. I know the truth now. You're Wyatt."

The Prism Master freezes. "What did you say?"

"You may have been born an osmos elf, but you were chosen to become a werewolf, same as I was. You discovered your mate would be Opal, the next quintessence. But around the same time, you also discovered that the real quintessence was Grayson. You'd be the beta to my alpha. So you and Opal came up with the plan for Grayson's sister to become a Rapunzel. What you didn't realize is that while it split Opal into a Rapunzel and witch, it would also break you into a man and a half-shifted wolf. That's Taryn.

The Prism Master pales. "No!"

"That's why you kept testing me," I continue. "You wanted to see if I'd figured out the truth. Because just as most of Opal's magic went into Jocasta, it didn't all go. Some stayed. And you never shared bites with your mate, so Opal didn't have much of a wolf."

"I don't have a wolf," says the Prism Master. "Not really."

"Because most of that magic went to Taryn. Most, but not *all*." When I next speak, I place alpha energy into my voice. "Free me and Grayson."

The Prism Master steps away. "No. You don't know how I've suffered. I helped Opal become Rapunzel because I wanted to please my fated mate. I had no idea that it would separate us forever. And now, you want me to spend the rest of my days watching you enjoy what I lost?"

"FREE US!"

The crystal that imprisoned me vanishes. "Set the rest of them free as well," I order.

The Prism Master throws himself against the mirror. "I made a wish! I told you to give me the life I deserve! That can't happen while these two are alive, let alone their friends."

A woman's voice echoes through the chamber. It's the mirror. "You've always been in line to get what you deserve."

A crystal juts up from the ground, heading for the Prism Master. This one doesn't encase him in a crystal dungeon, though. It spears the Prism Master through the heart. He slumps over, dead.

There's no time to process this turn of events. I look to Grayson. Per my order, she's now free from the crystal that encased her. Even so, the ribbons of power still wind between her and Lady R. Turning my hands into claws, I swipe at the lines of osmos magic with my talons. My strikes simply pass through the magical connection.

Even worse, Grayson's head slumps forward. Her

limbs look rubbery. The only thing keeping my vita upright are the very cords of power that are draining her life away.

Grayson doesn't have long.

GRAYSON

More ribbons of silver power extend from my palm to Lady R. The world around me collapses until all I can see is my sister.

"Shh, sweet Grayson," she coos. "It will all be over soon."

At those words, something deep inside me awakens. White-hot rage careens through my nervous system.

This is my life, mate and loved ones. I may not win, but I'll go down fighting.

When Dex and I tried to rejuvenate the Wulfhelm magic, we were joined via the Muster Tree. My green osmos power could then flow into Dex.

A realization appears. I'm connected to Lady R, same as she's linked to me. Giving up power isn't my only option.

I can take it back as well.

All I need is an extra power boost to reverse the flow of magic. And I know just how to do it. My right hand is still locked to Lady R with supernatural ribbons. With the little energy I have left, I shift my left hand into a wolf claw. Clenching my fist, I allow my talons to dig into my palm and draw blood.

Looking to Dex, I reach out with my bloody hand. I force out four words.

"We *can* do this."

Dex nods. All the love and determination in the universe shine in his eyes. He shifts his own right hand into a claw and clenches his fist. When he reaches for me, his own palm is bloody as well. I recall the realization from Ulliver and Hiriah, a few days and a million years ago.

The mating ceremony isn't about place or bites. It's powered by the exchange of blood.

Dex and I clasp our hands. The moment our blood touches, a lightning bolt of energy moves through me. Every muscle in my body stiffens.

Meanwhile, Lady R has been staring at the ribbons of magic. She now glances up and notices the chance between me and Dex. A smile quirks the corner of her mouth. "How sweet. You're holding hands as you die."

Sure, that's it.

My inner wolf howls inside me. Powers align in my soul. A new kind of magic arises.

Now, it's my turn to focus on the ribbons of power between me and Lady R. Before, flashing lights of magic moved along the ribbons, showing the shift of power from me to Lady R.

Those lights stop. The transfer of power ceases.

Lady R snaps her attention to me. "What are you trying to do?"

A new inner animal howls inside me. Fur erupts along my skin. My senses heighten. Smells are sharper. The ribbons of silver power appear impossibly bright. My muscles realign.

I look over to Dex. His body is changing as he takes on his wolf form.

Lady R inches closer. "Do you really think you can beat me? You're not a killer, Grayson."

More power and energy move through me. I meet my sister's gaze, dead on. When I speak, my voice carries a low growl. "I'm not a killer. I. Am. A. Wolf."

The full magic of my first shift courses through me. Through our connected hands and blood, I sense Dex's alpha power as well. With a burst of light, we take our true forms together.

We are wolves.

My body is tall, powerful and encased in gray fur. While Dex and I no longer hold hands, there's now a deeper connection. We are shifter mates. Our souls entwine.

The ribbons of power between me and Lady R alter again. This time, the bright lines of magic loop around my front before burrowing into my rib cage. I sense the connection in my heart. And I issue a command to my lost magic.

Come back. You are mine.

For the last few minutes, the ribbons had no longer flashed with the flow of power. Now they light up again, only this time, the energy moves from Lady R into me. Every corner of my soul becomes charged with the ultimate in osmos magic.

Lady R screams and curls over. "Stop!"

At this point, the flow of magic is too powerful. I couldn't stop the transfer, even if I wanted to.

A moment passes. Perhaps it's an eternity. When I'm aware again, I'm in the crystal chamber. Dex and I are both in our wolf forms.

What's left of Lady R lies before us. She's nothing but a skeleton in a red dress—a sight that reminds me of Alice and the Mad Hatter.

Lady R is gone.

The Prism Master is no more.
Our struggle could be done.
It's just beginning.

39

DEX

Grayson and I are in our wolf forms, standing in the center of the crystal chamber. Everyone we love is trapped. Magic swirls in and around us.

Pop, pop, pop!

An unmistakable noise sounds. A great round mirror appears nearby. The frame is carved with wolf heads. A new voice booms through the air. "What do you wish?"

This is a new mirror, created by Grayson's first spell as quintessence.

Fortunately, we now have experience with powerful mirrors. When it was her chance, Snow White chose servitude. Alice opted for destruction.

What Elise would do in this situation?

I don't think she'd simply ask for aid. It's one thing to

plead with a magic mirror for help. It's another to create a partnership. And as supernatural items go, these mirrors are rather touchy. The answer appears in a flash.

"We want you to join our pack," I reply. "Help us rebuild Wulfhelm and Refraction."

"Is that what you *both* wish?" asks the voice.

"Yes," confirms Grayson. "Very much."

"Granted."

Before, the ribbons of power had been winding around me and Wolf Grayson. Now they plunge inside us. I sense the fire of Wulfhelm and this new mirror magic.

There are no more instructions from the mirror. None are needed. What happens next is pure instinct.

Moving in unison, Wolf Grayson and I tilt our heads back and howl. A column of fire, both silver and emerald, surrounds both of us. We howl again. The pillar of magic shoots into the sky, coloring the clouds in green and silver.

Even more magic churns through us. This time, the power rolls out across the crystal chamber. Everything it touches changes. The original crystal mirror implodes. A cascade of sparkles settle over the land. All the crystals holding our loved ones vanish. The pups are freed, along with the teachers, Elise, the harpies, and Zoya. Even Taryn and Jocasta get loose.

Instinct keeps driving me and Wolf Grayson. We picture our lands healing. The mirror magic responds. Emerald and silver flames expand out from what was once the crystal chamber. The supernatural fire rolls over the countryside like ripples in a pond. Everywhere the power touches, the land is healed. Trees grow. Waterfalls tumble into fast-moving rivers. Ruined palaces become new again.

The magic keeps going. In my mind, I see the emerald and silver flames moving over Wulfhelm. The grounds are renewed. The city is repaired. Our Muster Tree sews itself back together again.

Pop, pop, pop!

As quickly as the power began, it ends. There's no more fire, but there is a repaired world.

I've never seen anything more beautiful.

Refraction

40

GRAYSON

In the story of Brutus and Vita, a Roman centurion founded a new island nation with his lady love. Dex told me how at one time, Wulfhelm lands were well protected. If an enemy set foot on our territory, a column of green fire would reach up to the skies.

As of today, those protective flames will rise again, only the fires will now be emerald and silver. If I hadn't seen the renewal with my own eyes, I'd have never believed such a thing was possible.

Yet, here it is. A sense of wonder overtakes everyone as we soak in this new world. The pups leap and yip in the tall grass. Harpies soar through the sky. Jacoby marvels at the flowers. Taryn and Jocasta hold hands as they scoop drinking water from a fresh stream. Zoya, the future Prism Queen, steps about in slow circles and smiles.

And my inner wolf helped to unlock these wonders. Perhaps that's the most—and least—surprising thing of all.

Wolf Dex nuzzles my fur. "Well?" he prompts.

"We did it," I say simply.

Wolf Dex grins. "That *we* did."

—The End—

Read on for a bonus appendix of book images!

The Fairy Tales of the Magicorum returns with Evil Queens and Goblin Kings

GRAYSON

DESCRIPTION - EVIL QUEENS AND GOBLIN KINGS

The Fairy Tales of the Magicorum series continues with EVIL QUEENS AND GOBLIN KINGS…

About EVIL QUEENS AND GOBLIN KINGS

Like all Magicorum, seventeen-year-old Avianna is supposed to follow a fairy tale life template. *Too bad hers is the evil queen from Snow White.* Even so, Avie makes herself the best evil queen in her coven. Mastering potions? Easy. Enduring a bitey pet raven? Bring on the enchanted Band-Aids. But there's one requirement Avie can't accept with a smile.

On her eighteenth birthday, Avie must marry the handsome-yet-creepy Ice White, CEO of Tundra Pharmaceutical. What a mess. The company is almost bankrupt and Ice's daughter, Snow, is more interested in clubbing with dwarves than actually helping out. To keep Tundra going, Avie must schmooze their top customer, the infamous Goblin Assegai. There she encounters the goblin prince, Kane, a guy who's kind, intelligent and drop-dead gorgeous. Sparks fly; questions appear.

For the first time, Avie considers breaking from her destiny as evil queen. But what would that mean for Tundra? Thousands rely on the company's life-saving potions. Bankruptcy could kill them. Not to mention how the hunters of Avie's coven regularly assassinate anyone who denies their fairy tale life template.

But now that Avie has a future worth fighting for, maybe it's time *the good girl* tries a little evil scheming…

Witches of the Magicorum

Modern fairy tales with sass, action, and romance

1. Evil Queens and Goblin Kings
2. Mad Hatters and Manhattan Heirs
3. Goose Girls and Ghost Magic

ALSO BY CHRISTINA BAUER

EVIL QUEENS AND GOBLIN KINGS

BOOK 1, WITCHES OF THE MAGICORUM

Looks like the evil queen in Snow White isn't so bad after all… Order today!

PIXIELAND DIARIES tells the story of sassy pixie Calla and 'her' elf prince, Dare.

APPENDIX

ACKNOWLEDGMENTS

If you're reading my freaking acknowledgements, chances are, I should thank you for something. So, for the record: you are awesome, dear reader.

That said, huge and heartfelt thanks must go out to my husband and son for their rock-solid support. Being an author means a lot of early mornings, late nights, long weekends, and never-ending patience. You two are the best guys in the universe, period.

After that, I must thank the extensive network of reviewers, friends and colleagues who helped me build my writing chops in general. Gracias.

Finally, deep affection goes out to my late, much loved, and dearly missed Aunt Sandy and Uncle Henry. You saw the writer in me, always. Thank you, first and last.

ABOUT CHRISTINA BAUER

Christina Bauer thinks that fantasy books are like bacon: they just make life better. All of which is why she writes romance novels that feature demons, dragons, wizards, witches, elves, elementals, and a bunch of random stuff that she brainstorms while riding the Boston T. Oh, and she includes lots of humor and kick-ass chicks, too. Christina lives in Newton, MA with her husband, son, and semi-insane golden retriever, Ruby.

Stalk Christina on Social Media

Blog:
http://monsterhousebooks.com/blog/category/
christina

Facebook:
https://www.facebook.com/authorBauer/

Instagram:
https://www.instagram.com/christina_cb_bauer/

Twitter:
@CB_Bauer

VLOG:
https://tinyurl.com/Vlogbauer

Web site:
www.bauersbooks.com

BONUS IMAGES

Dear Reader,

Every time I write a book, I build all sorts of stuff that doesn't end up directly on the page. Once the novel is done, I can't imagine any other story. Yet, while I'm doing it, I just want to slam my skull against a wall.

How can I lose such a great character or storyline?

For this book, I'm sharing some of the stuff which ended up on the cutting room floor of my imagination. Perhaps someday, these nuggets will appear in another book. For now, I hope you enjoy a wider view of Dex and Grayson's world!

- CB

PS. The Fairy Tales of the Magicorum returns with Evil Queens and Goblin Kings!

1

YOUNG DEX

This image goes along with an edit to the scene where Dex meets the future Prism Master at Fortune's Altar. Originally, I wanted to show young Dex interacting with the pack and scampering over the hills. However, the scene was already complex with the future Prism Master talking to the current Dex. Adding in Young Dex made it hard for me to follow, and I'm the freaking author.

I got a good young Dex pic out of the exercise, though.

DEX

2

CRIMSON CAP BROWNIES

There was a scene with young Dex before encountering the future Prism Master. In Grayson's journey through the mirror, there was a scene between a youthful version of herself and some sassy Crimson Cap Brownies. It was fun. It was silly. It just extended the scene in the mirror too long and lost all momentum for the book.

But the Crimson Cap Brownies are cute as Hell.

CRIMSON CAP BROWNIE

3

MAYOR PRIMROSE

This was another fully-realized series of scenes where Young Grayson and Elise visit a village to save some injured lupines. There would be a magical showdown with Mayor Primrose, who you'll see on the next page. This part of action-packed, full of adventure, and included more non-magical wolf puppies (and I firmly believe it's impossible to have too many puppies in any story.)

Sadly, this was becoming a book about Young Grayson.

Buh bye, Mayor Primrose! You are relegated to a sentence, but not forgotten.

MAYOR PRIMROSE

4

SIDHE ACADEMY

The Sidhe Academy is where Opal (aka the future Lady R) went to school. She skipped class and got sucked up to, often. I had teachers, students and the all-important librarian mapped out. Why? There was the great mystery of who had taken Opal's books... and how Grayson knew the way to cast mirrors.

Opal slowly changed her appearance from a regular osmos far into someone who really needed to lay off the make-up.

This was becoming the Sidhe Academy book. I had to cut the whole thing, although it was necessary to work this out in order for the story to keep moving.

Sidhe Academy

5

THE ESTUARY

I'd set up in previous books that Dex's family were vassals to Prince Jacoby. This involved mapping out the Estuary and the character of Dex's father. As I dove into this stuff, I came up with a whole series of encounters with Dex and his dad.

You may be shocked to discover that the book was veering into the My Blue Dad Hates Me book.

The next image shows you the Estuary.

THE ESTUARY

6

SHOAL

This is Dex's father, Shoal. Some kids are just selected by magic to become werewolves. Dex was one of those kids.

Let's just say that Shoal did not handle this well. Which is a shame. If he'd had the kid he expected, Shoal night have been a good father.

As it stands, he was a total dick.

SHOAL

THE KRAKEN

As one of Jacoby's vassal families, Dex's family cared for sea monsters. And although Dex didn't look like the other fae at the Estuary, he was pretty good with the mega creatures of the deep.

Dex's best water-bound buddy was the Kraken. Everyone else was terrified of the great sea beast, but Dex found the Kraken easy to get along with (if you ignored the fact that he never cleaned up the bones that were leftover after his every meal.)

Kraken

8

DAMASCUS AT FORT ZEMNI

This image went with a flashback to how Dex and Jacoby became friends. As you may know from other books, Jacoby's royal family loves to kill each other. Or in Jacoby's case, try to do so.

In this deleted scene, Jacoby's older brother Damascus tried to level Fort Zemni, which is the castle where Jacoby was currently residing. Dex happened by and helped Jacoby repulse his brother. They stayed fast friends ever since.

Again, this was a good bit and filled with action, but it wasn't driving the core story forward.

DAMASCUS AT FORT ZEMNI

JOCASTA

For the final scene of the book, I was going to have Jocasta break free from the mirror pendant and kick ass. It was a good battle, but it was stealing Grayson's thunder.

It was fun to see Jocasta in her ass kicking boots, though.

JOCASTA

TARYN

Last but not least, here's Taryn. I've wanted to include a picture of him from the beginning, but there never was a good spot. This book was no exception.

Yet, here he is in all his half-wolf glory.

Huzzah, Taryn!

TARYN

CLOSING

So, there you have it—some of the stuff that ends up on my virtual cutting room floor of world building.

You may wonder: do I ever think, *screw it*, and keep the stuff in there anyway because it's cool? I try, but then I get writer's block. Simply put, my inner editor won't let go of an errant puzzle piece that's ruining what it sees as the bigger picture.

Over the years, I've learned that it's easier and faster to just cut something that isn't working. I save a draft somewhere else and can always add it back in if necessary. It rarely is, however. Plus, I write enough books that the sequence will find a home somewhere else eventually.

Hope you enjoyed this review!
Now, I must get back to writing…
CB

9 781956 114454